New U

by
Daniel DiPrinzio

PublishAmerica
Baltimore

First printing

All characters in this book are fictitious, and any resemblance to real persons, living or dead, is coincidental.

PublishAmerica has allowed this work to remain exactly as the author intended, verbatim, without editorial input.

ISBN: 978-1-4489-7997-4
PUBLISHED BY PUBLISHAMERICA, LLLP
www.publishamerica.com
Baltimore

Printed in the United States of America

for you

Table of Contents

"There was never any more inception than there is now,
Nor any more youth or age than there is now,
And will never be any more perfection than there is now,
Nor any more heaven or hell than there is now."

—Walt Whitman, *Leaves of Grass*

"Here we are."
—Lamken philosophy

New U

Prologue

Sometime in their twenties, Los and his best friend, Mas, were chosen by their fellow Lamkens to climb Mount Laddis and throw into the volcano's mouth prayers of the primitive people. The islanders had little food, and less hope. They prayed that the gods would deliver unto them a new life.

During their ascent, Mount Laddis suddenly belched, ejaculating a shower of fire.

Los scrambled up a crag while all around him hell swarmed. He watched in horror as a molten river swallowed the mountain, and Mas disappeared in lava.

When the red-black waves subsided, Los was unharmed, but stranded. For 10 days he sat atop the crag, convinced he would die. But on the 11th day, Mas appeared in a dream, astride a winged, white horse.

"Mas!" Los cried. "I bow before you! Do you come to tell me tales from beyond this life? Are you here to answer my pleas about how I can get down from here? Is there any chance you have something to eat?"

"Listen to me very carefully, Los. What I am to tell you will shape the destiny of our island."

"What about the horse?" Los asked. "How closely are you attached to it? Because I haven't eaten anything for who knows how long and I'm—"

"Los! Listen to me. I don't have much time. I present to you the fate of Lamken. This island is to become a New Utopia, the most powerful place on earth. A garden of plenty, where all will have what they wish."

"What? How? And when? Anytime soon? Because I'd kill for a drink of water."

"Men in suits will descend from the sky. You might be wondering what 'suits' are. They're two- or three-piece outfits of clothing, sometimes worn with a tie. These men—the most powerful in the world—will unknowingly teach our people the way to New Utopia."

"What's New Utopia? And will there be a feast?"

"Lamkens will one day control a sun," Mas continued. "Once the power of this sun is harnessed, its beams able to focus on anything we wish, these men in suits will bow before us. In order to control this sun, four Lamken women will be sent to bear fruit in another land. The fruit will provide information on how to set controls of the sun. The fruit also will find a gray man to secure the island. It is only when this man is met that the time to overtake the suits will be at hand. Do you understand?"

"I think I do, sure. We'll rule the world when fruit tells us how to control the sun and somebody comes to secure the island. That about sum it up?"

"Pretty much."

"Great," said Los. "Now how am I going to get down from here?"

Part I

Chapter One

Breakfast

The Decision Makers might not have known everything, but they knew the Decisions they made were right.

—Grey Reflections

All across America people woke, the East Coast rising first before the domino effect of stacked time zones pulled the rest of the country out of bed.

Many greeted the day with Beano Machino[1] coffee.

Laborers put on boots.

Office workers donned ties.

First grade teachers prepared lessons on the letter C.

Most of the people, even with more distractions and methods of entertainment than all other people in history combined, were dreadfully bored.

"Are you worried about somebody breaking into your home just as you turn on 'Cutting Rugs—and Skin[2]?' Unfortunately, the world we live in now has made this once-unlikely scenario not only possible, but probable. At Dubs Home Security Systems, we understand the dynamic shift our society has undergone. And somebody's got to protect you. Call 1-888-LOC-DOWN for an estimate on what it would take to fortify your home. Let us worry about the threats and dangers so you don't have to."

Neither Jeff nor Celia paid any conscious attention to the television during Dubs' commercial. If they had, Jeff, out of insecurity, might have said something derogatory about Dubs, who he'd known growing up but never thought too much of. And even though Dubs made less in profit per year than Jeff, Dubs was on television, which was Celia's never-fail aphrodisiac.

The commercial contained the rapper/actor Nay Need Nadas's hit song, "Rollin' on Dubs," written as a celebration of his tricked-out car. Jeff and Celia, being suburban-semi-down with hip-hop, knew the song, and if they were out and had had enough to drink, or driving by themselves, they may have rapped along with it. Dubs bought the one line, "We're rollin' on dubs," for $50,000 (and a free installment in Nay Need Nadas' mini-mansion in North Jersey), with the hope of increasing sales. He was banking on the song drawing rap fans to his business, and scaring those wary of the rap generation into protecting themselves against people in baggy pants.

While the commercial didn't generate a sharp increase in profit for Dubs, it did spike record sales for Nay Need Nadas.

The television was always on whenever at least one of them was home, doing its best to dominate discussions. They couldn't eat without it, and if not for the sleep timer, images would flicker all night. They didn't spend all of their time watching it; they just enjoyed the comfort.

"It doesn't matter what I eat," Jeff said as he came in from the bathroom. "Everything goes right through me."

"Then maybe you shouldn't have any eggs," Celia said, grabbing the half-and-half from the refrigerator. "Just have toast with a little butter. I don't even know if you should have coffee. Sometimes that makes me go."

"Well, there's no way I'm cutting that out."

"Drink tea instead."

"I don't get the same boost from tea."

Celia pulled the pot out from the bottom of the Beano Machino Coffee Maker. As she poured two cups, a drop hit the burner and hissed.

"What time do you have to be in?"

"Ten," Celia answered.

"I have darts tonight; do you want me to bring back something for dinner?"

"Sure."

Halfway through his coffee, "Ohhh; ohhhhhh," Jeff grabbed his belly and two sections of the newspaper and headed toward the bathroom.

"I really think you should cut back on coffee," Celia said, opening to the paper's celebrity section, the only one she read.

Cecelia should have been a celebrity, the American dream. It's a shame she wasn't, because she knew exactly what she'd do, where she'd live, who she'd befriend. She'd even seen her nervous breakdown and knew what her press statement would say (she vowed to always write her own statements, no matter the situation), thanking her fans for their continued devotion, prayers, and support, and letting them know they were the reason for her comeback. Dedicating her life to stardom was something she'd put over family and health. After all, she knew as well as anyone how much run-of-the-mill people needed celebrities.

Everything had assured her she'd be famous. She was the most popular girl in elementary and high school[3]. A decent athlete. Not so bright, but it didn't matter; she got by quite fine. Everyone wanted to help her.

She was very hot, yes, but more importantly, had that which separates regular people from the ones who are talked about. It didn't matter what they said, what rumors spread through school halls and floated around college bars; she ate it all up.

Her parents met at a Paul Simon concert in the late '70s. Celia's mother's family was from Philadelphia's Main Line Lower Merion section, though I never found out how they landed there.

The two concertgoers, between puffs of a joint, decided that night to marry and have a daughter, who they'd name Cecelia. It wasn't clear whether they said that they'd tell their daughter the song was written for her, and it's also unclear as to who first began telling this tale; but the daughter believed it, and argued with schoolmates who called her a liar. When Celia came home upset and friendless, her mother and father told her the other little girls and boys were jealous and beneath her, and Celia needn't worry about them. Her parents were only trying to raise the little girl's spirits.

Blonde hair she no longer allowed past her shoulders, hazel eyes, between 5'8" and 6'1", depending on the shoe. B cups, a torso she never thought attractive, which was almost as long as her legs. She also fretted about her ankle bones, and the way she thought they jutted out in back of her Achilles heel.

But Celia's popularity peaked her second year in college. There wasn't any defining moment or particular event that halted everything; the progression simply ended. And she felt it, like a boy who stops growing before he hits 16.

Now, some people would say that she at least had a good run, and was able to enjoy her popularity. They were, of course, the same people who never tasted fame, and had no idea how hard it was—some would even say unfair—to have to ingratiate yourself back into general population.

After college, she replaced popularity with calories and light beer, Pilates and martinis. But she never deferred the dream of TMZ. When she was 25, what she thought was her big break came when she was chosen among the hundreds of thousands[4] of applicants as a contestant on Survivor. On the flight to the island, as she strategized and sized up other contestants, a large flock of birds following a mentally deranged leader flew directly into the plane's twin engines, and everything with wings went down about 100 yards from shore. It was a skimmer plane, and never rose more than 20 or 30 feet off of the ground. Nobody died, but the cameras and production equipment were ruined, and they had to cancel that season's show. The producers wished more than anything that somebody, somewhere, could have recorded the plane going down. They knew the ratings would have been astronomical. So they did the next best thing. They created a reenactment, a tv movie based on true events, with "contestants" stuck on the island for a few weeks without food and shelter. In the movie, people formed teams, or tribes, and tried to sabotage the other groups' supplies.

The ratings were astronomical.

After the crash and before the movie, Celia still believed this was her big break, and pleaded with producers through unreturned phone calls and e-mails that they should cast her in the role of Cecelia. After all, who could play her better than herself?

She even showed up at the producers' office in New York, where she was told by a production assistant younger than her that while she certainly would have been in the running for the role, she wasn't psychologically or emotionally stable enough to take part in such a rigorous shooting schedule—after all, she had just survived a plane crash.

It was a year before Celia could function properly in society, her psychological and emotional instability resulting from the crash of her dream not becoming reality. She slept late each day and spent her parents' money on items that she'd sometimes throw away before unwrapping.

She didn't count that year in her life, believing everybody deserved a year off. Celebrities got them, didn't they?

When she turned 28, though, frightened by the prospect of loneliness and, even worse, going to another set of holiday parties without modeling some expensive stone (or two), she decided to act. Or react, at least. Jeff came along, took her to restaurants with three-and-a-half dollar signs in a food rating guide[5]. When he asked to marry her, the ring was more than appropriate, and they honeymooned in Fiji.

She never took his last name. She hated it.

Jeff was a nice guy. Something that could spell death for men, but in this situation, a pair of queens in a jacks-or-better poker game—enough to get you in the hand.

When Jeff turned 32 and Celia 31, they bought a two-story brick move-right-in home. There was an ideal place for a garden, if only one of them gardened. Jeff mowed his own lawn, and during the first winter, kids on the street threw semi-frozen Tastykakes at his car. A cream-filled chocolate cupcake stuck to the driver's side headlight, and was a bitch to get off.

Celia, by the way, was not alone in thinking that she should have been a celebrity. At this particular time in America, many many people felt as if they should, could and would be a celebrity. After all, you didn't need talent or skill to be famous. All you had to do was get in front of enough cameras.

Many many people thought they deserved it, that it was only a matter of time. And I guess they did deserve it, at least as much as the next guy. Many many people were disappointed.

* * *

At this time I was in a relationship with Julie. Or, should I say, getting out of a relationship with Julie.

Here we are.

"It doesn't matter what we do, how we live our lives," I said. "We're all going to die with regrets."

"I know a lot of people who say they live exactly as they want, that they wouldn't change a thing," she said.

—"have you seen my shoes?" I asked.

"they're wherever you left them," she huffed—

"And you believe them," I said, returning to the original conversation. "And why not—they're not necessarily lying. I mean, they believe what they're saying is the truth. But they don't know what they're talking about."

"You know, Grey, I hate it when you talk stupid," she said. "You don't know anything about anyone else's mind. You're always talking about how you can hardly figure yourself out…"

"I say I can't do that."

"Right, whatever, just listen." She sighed, rolled her eyes to milk the rebuff. "And how you can't do that, but you have no problem figuring other people out. Now that's just stupid, Grey."

—"what about my wallet?" I asked.

"I don't know! I told you, I'm not picking up after you anymore," she said—

"But I can make generalities about other people," I continued, "because I'm a person, and I know some things humans go through. But I can't figure myself out—it's like how you can't judge something's speed and something else…."

"What?"

"I don't know; someone said it. The uncertainty principle."

"Here we go, more bullshit," she said, tossing her cell phone and keys and Tic Tacs in her purse.

"No, what I mean is, we're all going to have regrets, because even if we choose what we want, or think we want, some part of us will always want what we didn't choose. That's regret."

"That's not regret."

"That's regret."

She couldn't think of anything suitable to say. "You're such an asshole, you know that? You don't even know how much of an asshole you are. Here are your goddamn keys," she said, throwing them at me. I didn't catch them.

I had a habit of leaving things everywhere. In a word, I was careless. I'd like to think that now, many years later, I've gotten past that habit. Of course, maybe I haven't, and it's only because there hasn't been anyone to yell at me to pick things up in what seems like so long that I think I've overcome that habit. But I at least *admit* that I was guilty of the carelessness for which Julie reprimanded me, and that's usually a big part in overcoming it.

Julie needed to have her living space neat and clean, something she attributed to her father not buying her a Blizzard at Dairy Queen after she fell on the ice during the Little Misses Figure Skating Expo when she was 13. She revealed this on the one and only trip we made to a relationship counselor just before this story's beginning. We stopped going once we found out the counselor was on her fourth marriage.

We used to watch Good Day Philadelphia in the morning while we got ready for work, but Julie put a stop to that, saying she'd rather talk instead of watch tv. I think the real reason is because she'd end up doing more watching than getting ready for work, and was late several times.

I must admit that, although there wasn't anything particularly exciting on the morning shows, I found myself watching more and more, and also was late for work several times.

We found a way to argue about almost everything. I knew that was expected in any relationship, especially between lovers, especially when living together; but I think we may have went at it more than normal.

On some levels, I enjoyed arguing, and believed with every little sinew in my heart that the ability to argue successfully was necessary in any coupling. Of course, Julie disagreed, which only drew me to her. I didn't like how she always interpreted arguments as fights, and when I'd try and tell her the difference, we'd start fighting—*arguing*—about that.

We didn't really fight, though. Real fighting was between Julie's cousin, Jill, and her boyfriend, Jack.

Jill and Jack both smoked crack, and climbed up any hill to get it. Jill was a rare crackhead, utterly obese. Jack better fit the mold, skinny like an icicle. He constantly told her she needed to smoke more to lose weight (never offering her any of his, of course), but it didn't matter how much crack she smoked. She gained weight brushing her teeth. Though orca-like, she had somewhat of a cute, porcelain doll face. Such a shame it was always contorted in a grimace or snarl. She and Jack fought over crack, money, when one or both were suffering from withdrawal—but never like when it was over food.

Before Julie and I moved into our apartment, we hung out at Jill and Jack's place a lot, which Jack's parents, a detached couple who owned a couple of car dealerships, paid for, with the tacit agreement that the tenants never show up at the parents' home or any of the car dealerships.

One night, I walked into the kitchen for a glass of water. Jill was making grilled cheeses for her and Jack. Two sandwiches were on a plate, and she was finishing a second for herself. Jack swallowed his in about three bites, and for whatever reason, took a bite out of one of Jill's. Without saying a word, Jill took Jack's head and smashed it against the microwave cart. After Jack stopped the bleeding (the fat bitch insults flowing as freely as the blood, with Jill calmly gulping down her meal), he went upstairs and ripped the heads off of her stuffed animals.

Another time, Jill kicked Jack out of a car going 25 miles per hour because he ate two handfuls of her French fries after she warned him not to take more than one. After she leaned over and shut the door, she changed the radio station. I was in the backseat.

I mention these two people to show relativity, a concept which surely was known by humans for a long long time, but wasn't made famous and ready-made until about 100 years ago by a smart-as-all-hell physicist.

The actual theory of relativity is much too complex to explain to the average person, and much too complex for me to completely comprehend. But Albert Einstein, the smart-as-all-hell physicist who made the theory famous and ready-made, simplified relativity for the average folk: "When a man sits with a pretty girl for an hour, it seems like a minute. But let him sit on a hot stove for a minute, and it's longer than any hour."

So as not to sound sexist, "woman," "hot guy," and "her" can easily be substituted for "man," "pretty girl," and "him." Relativity does not discriminate.

Chapter Two

Working Stiff

It's not what you bet—it's how you bet!

—Peppercorn

"Yo Grey."

"Peppercorn?"

"What are you doing?"

"I'm at work. What're you doing?"

"I'm at the track."

"Why aren't you at work?"

"I am."

"I mean at your job."

"Oh, I'm not going back there anymore."

"What? Why?"

"I had enough of that. But don't fret. I'm going to install home security systems."

"You're going to install home security systems?" I asked.

"Yes indeedie," Peppercorn said. "Yeah, give me 20 on the four at Belmont and key it over the one and the six for five dollars."

"Peppercorn; c'mon man, I'm at work."

"What do you want me to do?" he asked. "The horses are going in the gate."

Everybody was always doing something with cell phones. In fact, there's a good chance that you're fiddling with one right now.

The average cell phone conversation was about three minutes, just to pass some time for whoever was calling. Text message conversations, though, could last all day.

"Dubs wants me to come in this afternoon," he said.

"You know what? You'll probably do alright."

"I surely hope."

"You coming tonight?"

"Where?"

"HaL's," I said. "It's darts night."

"You got a better shot at getting pregnant," he said.

"Alright. Listen, I have to—"

"Yeah, stand up baby, ride it, ride it, c'mon be the best, get it four get it four get it four get it four—"

I had to stay on to see if it hit.

"—get it four get it four whooooo we GOT IT!"

He hung up on me.

Peppercorn was a gambler, which isn't the same as saying he gambled. As with anything, it took him a while to get good, and he lost a lot of money in those first couple of years. He liked to say that he wasn't losing money, but paying for lessons. He also said those early losses were well worth every dollar spent.

Because when he lost, he'd see why he lost. Maybe not right after; but he was always respectfully retrospective in his picks, and if he couldn't find something about the pick's present, he'd look at its past, see what kind of times the horses ran in their previous three races on grass after moving down from a $35,000 claiming race to a $18,000 starter allowance race, or what the Broncos' road trend was against AFC South opponents after Denver was coming off a favored victory in November; and patterns began to appear.

His father was a meteorologist, feeding reports to local news stations. He and several other weather predictors gambled on their picks. The first bet Peppercorn's father made won four dollars because nobody thought they'd get two inches of rain. As a result, he started studying odds, and made a surprising amount of money for a gambling meteorologist. Not I'll-go-out-and-get-me-a-Lincoln-kind-of-money, but Honey-c'mon-get-Peppercorn-ready-we're-going-out-to-dinner-again or Peppercorn-check-this-out-I-got-season-tickets money.

Peppercorn's father didn't do it for the action, though he certainly enjoyed that. He did it because it was a smart thing to do. He won money by following the three rules of his system: always put the odds in your favor, only bet best bets, and remain disciplined to the first two rules.

I don't know the official statistics on this, but I'd venture to say he was one of the best handicapping meteorologists who ever lived.

He never wanted his son to think that gambling was cool, and hid his method of side income from Pepper. Hid it well, as Pepper never knew. But if he wouldn't have hid it as well as he did, or if he'd sat down and talked to him about it, Peppercorn might not have lost as much those first couple of years. He'd have hit the ground running, evened out the playing surface with bookkeepers and oddsmakers. But Pepper found there is no teacher like experience.

Much more than his father, Peppercorn loved gambling. He said, "The next best thing to gambling and winning is gambling and losing. Action makes up for a lot."

And it's not like Peppercorn could have avoiding gambling. After all, it was his destiny.

Smooth-talking motherfucker Peppercorn was, too. He had two beach houses to stay at for free during the summer, both female owners knowing of the other, neither minding. Nor did they care when he brought guests, who were often female. Peppercorn always pulled whomever he was smooth-talking aside to speak in low tones with perfect fluctuation. His eyes were as influential as his mouth when he talked, sugar-coating the words so it didn't matter what he said. Whenever he was at a ballgame or concert, his seat was upgraded.

Though he was an all-star at handicapping sports betting, Peppercorn wasn't any good at sports in school. Or going to school at all. Though he was captain of the hooky team.

A shade under six feet, though he could cross that boundary depending on what shoe he wore. Usually had an unshaven face, but never seemed unkempt. Eyes had a cowboy squint, though he grew up and, except for a couple of trips to Vegas, lived his entire life in the Philadelphia area.

He was lean, had cropped black hair, and, though people didn't always notice it, quite a pleasant bodily odor.

Peppercorn had a system, too—"It's not what you bet, it's *how* you bet."

As good as he was, Peppercorn, like most gamblers, needed other sources of income. And it usually didn't come in the form of a steady job. So he hustled.

Or scammed, depending on which word you'd rather use.

He was the Jackson Pollack of hustles. He'd whip up scams that seemed, on the surface, so easy that anyone could do them. But when you looked a little closer, you saw angles that you never saw before, like:

A credit card scam, undertaken with a friend who worked at a car dealership and had access to people's financial information. They applied for a business credit card, usually American Express. Pepper either called the company right away, or they called him to verify some personal information, which he had memorized. ("I don't mess around with any paper trail, man. Gotta have it all in the noggin.") He'd then ask that the card be sent to a different address, because he was out of town. Now, the address again had to be somewhere that couldn't be traced back to him, and this is the one part—actually, I'm sure there were other parts, but this was at least one part—of the story I don't know how they got around—and Pepper or his partner scooped up the card at that address. Once in his possession, Pepper made one or two large cash advances, then destroyed the card and any evidence. They only did this with people who were financially secure and who had gone into the dealership a year or two before, in the hope that by the time they found out they had been the victims of fraud, they couldn't pinpoint exactly where their sensitive information had been stolen.

A sex dominatrix online scam, where Pepper posed as a female dominatrix in chat rooms and told men—mostly married, middle-aged men—that they were her slave, and demand that they send "her" money. Several wanted her to say that she would stomp on their testicles. Deposits flooded his PayPal account. One user, with the name Crybaby_Yitzie, sent more than $1,000. "I couldn't believe it!" he said to me. "And I'm not even robbing anyone—I'm just telling them to send me money!" As a matter of fact, Peppercorn made more productive use of the Internet than most people I knew. "It really is amazing what you can do on that Internet," he'd say. "It's opened up a whole new world for hustlers. There is no such thing as a dry town, because you can go global. And very big, if you have the right con and know the right people."

A merchandise scam, where a business was established—sometimes online—and merchandise ordered via credit, which he'd pay for, establishing trust with wholesalers. After first lining up buyers, he quickly shipped the products for the same price he paid, making no profit. (And with no markup, finding buyers was the easy part.) But once he ordered and paid for items from several suppliers, he'd order the largest amount he could from all of them, never pay, and sell the merchandise for half the price. When the suppliers went after the money, there was nobody to call; the business no longer existed, and everybody was gone.

Some would say that my closest friend was a criminal, but I wouldn't. He was more ethical than the government and most corporations, because he at least admitted what he did.

My other friend[6] was a systems analyst. I was a fact-checker who was about to become a security system installer.

We all gotta be something.
Here we are.

* * *

Jeff and I worked for the same group of very rich people at a large mortgage company in the PIMBCO[7] building in Center City Philadelphia. I used computers to check if information we used and released was accurate. My job was important, I guess, because facts were facts, and if something didn't have the privilege of being factual, it was my responsibility to expose the info as the liar it was.

Jeff corrected problems that computers inevitably developed. He walked people through steps over the phone if the computer was only acting up a bit, or made a cubicle-call for computers that needed more individualized attention. A psychiatrist for Apples and Dells. I guess that's why he was a systems analyst, not a systems fixer or checker.

Jeff's job was, in many ways, deemed as significantly more important, which is why he made significantly more money.

"And you know, Grey," Jeff began, "I didn't think it was going to happen to me, with me and Celia, didn't want it to happen to us, but our sex life has pretty much dwindled to a PG-rated movie. I'm lucky if I get a glimpse of her through the shower door. You know those fuzzy images you see when tv stations block out nudity? That's as good as it gets for me now."

We were in the coffee room, an oversized filing closet with one Beano Machino pot that spit grainy coffee which always managed to get cold in about two minutes. This was one of the few places where you could expect privacy, since the coffee was so terrible nobody ever came in here.

"Basically, she rations it out to me now. And, I mean, I'm not saying that I'm some sort of sex guru or anything, but we've only been married for a couple of years. This shouldn't happen so soon. I mean, she always used to enjoy it...."

"Why don't you try to, um, spice things up?" I asked.

"What, like costumes, role playing, that sort of thing?"

"I don't know. Sure, why not."

I tried to keep things light, because Jeff was a nervous type. In fact, his short, neat haircut that was not-so-slowly retreating from the front of his head, tucked-in shirts, sneakers, and chewed fingernails stuttered "nervous systems analyst." I didn't want to cause him any more worry or stress by adding any weight to his problem.

"We can't do that," he said. "Then we start depending on that? It'll start with costumes and role playing, and the next thing you know, there's a sheep in my room. It's not the act that needs spicing up; it's the situation."

"Well, if you change your mind, I know where you can get a good deal on livestock."[8]

Lunchtime. Recess for grown-ups. The one hour of the working day I'd start thinking about as soon as I got in. Whether I'd have the *Inquirer*[9] all to myself, if I'd have to settle for the sports, or if the new lady in back braces would horde it near her prunes and sauerkraut and who the hell knows what else she ate.

Today, I snatched the paper when Back Brace was in the bathroom, probably from eating all those prunes. Jeff and I sat outside in the courtyard with its eight steel caged tables and benches. PIMBCO had designed the patio as sort of a sidewalk café, with the aim of giving employees a place of sanctuary where they could enjoy the outdoors while they ate, smoked, or argued on a cell phone. The higher-ups had decided that this was a great idea for boosting employee morale, which would allow them to skimp on raises and bonuses. Now, though, weeds had sprouted through the cement cracks and nobody bothered cleaning up the pigeon shit that polka-dotted the black tables.

"Listen to this," I said, reading from the national news section. "Just outside of Boone, Iowa, an oil tanker was carjacked at gunpoint at a truck stop. As the carjacker fled, the driver, a card-carrying member of the NRA, pulled his weapon, and a shootout ensued. Though the carjacker was able to get away from the driver, when he pulled over a couple hundred yards away, *he* was carjacked at gunpoint! Apparently, the original carjacker had run out of bullets, which is why there wasn't a second shootout. The tanker was found more than 100 miles away, completely empty. Authorities are urging people to report anyone wearing oil-covered clothes, or those who go more than three days without complaining about the price of gas."

"Hm," Jeff said. "What happened to the original carjacker?"

"Oh, the driver, Joe Lannutti, caught up and killed him. The town is honoring Lannutti next week—the mayor's giving him a key to the city."

"I'm surprised stuff like that doesn't happen more often," Jeff said.

The country was in a crisis. With everybody running around, and things happening 24 hours a day, energy was in high demand. And although it couldn't be created or destroyed, it certainly could be bought and sold. People paid a lot for it, though the more they used, the more they needed.

And gasoline—whew! It cost people more and more to drive to work, which is where they needed to get so they could put gas in their cars.

People slurped up so much at the pump the nipples of the oil industry became chafed by so much sucking.[10]

People complained, and got mad, and yelled, and kicked tires, and said they were getting fucked, but then they'd drive home and get distracted by something or other, and forget about it until they had to fill up again.

Here we are.

The patio gave us a nice glimpse of the park across the street, which was, due to May's fine weather, filled with young professionals typing on laptops or chatting on cell phones or punching buttons on palm pilots or fiddling with iPods, and college students doing much the same while offering a glimpse of themselves in shorts, sweatpants, and tight tops.There were girls up to their mother's hips in tight sweatpants with words like 'squeeze' and 'pink' and 'huggable' and 'angel in training—just wait', which really made some men with a love of reading feel dirty.

Sunlight danced through the trees and speckled the ground like a giant disco ball. Shadows climbed up the brick and concrete walls and moved on down the line.

"Aren't you hungry?" I asked.

"Yeah."

"Well, there's food in front of you. Unless it's one of those foods that jumps into people's mouths, it's not gonna jump into your mouth."

"I'm trying to watch what I eat, I guess. I've been having problems going to the bathroom. I mean, I've been having problems about going to the bathroom too much. So I'd rather wait until I got home. At least this way I can relax."

"I see. Are you gonna eat those chips?"

"Nah, take em." "Oh man," Jeff said.

"What?"

"I'll be right back. I have to go to the bathroom."

"Doody calls,"[11] I said. I laughed. Sometimes I cracked myself up.

"Okay," Jeff said, returning to the table.

"Why don't you go to the doctor?"

"I don't want any prodding or poking going on in that area. You know what I mean?"

"Maybe you should. At least it'll be some action for you."

"How's Julie?" he asked.

Julie worked at a law office. She ordered sausage pizza from the lunch cafeteria, but took all the sausage pieces off. She just wanted the smoked flavor.

Julie was bigger than me, but in no way large. About 5'9", though she almost always wore heels, which pushed both her height and backside up a little higher. She was thick, but in no way fat. Every part of her was soft, but not mushy. It was a delicate balance.

Full teardrop breasts. Raspy voice. Her collarbones stuck out like wire hangers underneath a shirt, which she used to think so unattractive until her college years, when she embraced and flaunted them with style. Always kept her hair long, and her skin a dark tan.

We met on the street about two years before this story began. I had only been at my job for a few months, and took a walk during my lunch hour. Figured I'd stop at Angelo's lunch cart for a cheesesteak. As soon as I'd reached into the little metal window for the sandwich, I saw through a crowded sidewalk this young woman bending forward, picking up a sheaf of papers. I remember thinking how it was like the Discovery Channel detailing how animals mate on the Serengeti, the female simply bending over and showing the male her wares. Then I remembered how the last time I got a woman wet was when I spilled a soda on that lady at the movies, and the next thing I knew, I was on my knees, helping her scoop up the papers.

"Hi," I said, giving her the best opening line I could think of. "Saw you could, uh, maybe use a little help."

"Fucking asshole knocked all this shit out of my hands," she said without glancing at me. "Slammed right into me and kept on going. Didn't even notice. On the fucking phone. Oh, Christ, could you get those?" she pointed (still without glancing at me) to a manila folder flipping end over end toward the street.

I scuttled like a crab to the curb and reached for the folder. Just as I had my hand on it, somebody hurrying to cross before Don't Walk stopped flashing got an extra boost from my wrist, on which he came down quite unapologetically.

"Shit!" I yelled. "Goddamn!"

"Yeah, you believe these people?" she said with a smile. (Good-looking women have no greater weapon in their arsenal than that first smile. Well, maybe not *no* greater weapon; but the smile packs quite a punch.) She offered a hand, and I reached up with my right, the one that wasn't run over. "Oh, I meant for you to hand me the folder," she said, still smiling.

"Oh," I said, and still on my ass, gave it to her.

"Just kidding," she said, taking the folder. "Here." She reached down with her free hand and helped me up.

"Thanks. Yeah, nice crowd today, huh? Run you right over without looking to see if you're okay. I mean, they don't even throw a 'Sorry' or 'Scuse me' at you. I don't need the full 'Excuse me'; a simple 'Scuse' and I'd have been okay."

She laughed, and my hand felt a lot better.

Here we are.

We slept together the next night, and I fell for her. Not just the sex, though that was a huge part of it. I'd never had sex like that before. It was wild, it was connective, it made me feel like the stable's stud.

Though at times, sexually, she bent my mind a bit.

For instance, I'm a one-on-one kind of guy. I believe that there are enough variations of the ol' in and out to keep two young sexually actives sexually active, for at the very least the first year or so. A couple of weeks into it, right after we finished each other, she turned to me and proposed that we invite Carlos from upstairs into our next session.

"What?" I asked. "You're joking, right?"

"Why not?" she countered, lighting a cigarette. "I don't think he'd have a problem with it. And besides, the worst thing he could say is no."

"Actually, the worst thing he could say is yes. I'd prefer it if, during sex, the only people present are the ones who absolutely have to be here. Let's keep it a very exclusive club, okay? Besides, I'm not into, you know, guys like that. Guys at all, I mean. And I don't want you to be with any other guys. Even the ones people wonder about. Especially the ones people wonder about. You know…it's…we're with each other now, right?"

"Okay, what about Mrs. McCarthy?"

"Mrs. McCarthy? From down the street?"

"Yeah. What's wrong with her?"

"Well, only the fact that she's got two kids—in college!"

"But she keeps herself in good shape."

"She does keep herself in good shape. That I'll give you. All right. Then how about the fact that, uh, *she's married*?"

"Soon to be separated. And she happens to be lonely and bored."

"How do you know?"

"I ran into her the other morning."

"And she told you all this?"

"In so many words. Hand me that ashtray." I leaned over and grabbed the tray from the floor on my side, and held it out. "And I think her joining us for a nice night is a good idea," she said, flicking ashes all over my wrist. "We'll make dinner, have some wine, maybe smoke a joint, and then who knows. I really think it would do her good; not to mention I think she'd thoroughly enjoy it."

"Well, I'm sorry to have to be the wet blanket on this one, but I don't think that's somewhere I'm gonna head to, if you can dig me. I mean, you're not getting tired of this already, are you?"

"No, not at all," she said, stubbing out the cigarette. "Not at all." Before she'd finished exhaling the smoke, she'd, uh, re-assumed the position.

Much like arguing, sex in a relationship between lovers is pretty damn important. You don't want, especially if you're young, a problem to work its way into the bedroom. Because once that happens, all your other problems are magnified tenfold. If your partner doesn't like the way you slurp your soup, or the fact that you never put the seat down, or maybe that you're too demanding, it won't make a difference if you can knock it out during the horizontal—or vertical—shuffle. Because a nice orgasm supersedes a whole lot.

At the same time, the two of you can agree on everything in the world, but if there's a disconnect in the sex life, your relationship is sure to change. It's possible to still be close friends, but it's a little more difficult maintaining that friendship when they can visualize their genitals in your mouth whenever they want.

Chapter Three

Working for the Weekend

Selfishness may be a surefire cure for a temporary bout of depression or boredom, though just as often is a cause of such things.

—Grey Reflections

With jobs, relationships, and American boredom and futility, nothing helped people get through life like drugs.

Almost everybody was on something, and caffeine, alcohol, and cigarettes were the most popular. I doubt it was a coincidence that they were three of the legal ones.

Sure, illegal drugs were a problem, and made a mess of people, but legal drugs dispensed from pharmacies weren't the safest, either. All kinds of drugs were manufactured every day in laboratories and kitchens, and young and old lined up to gulp them down. As money makers went, drugs were right on the heels of sex, violence, energy, and foods that looked like Jesus.

* * *

Julie was already at the bar when I got there. As of recently, that was new. Before, she'd wait until I got done and pick me up at work. Now, I took the train to HaL's, whose Friday night happy hour drew a big crowd, with young professionals from the city, college students from any of the five universities in a 10-mile radius, and men in their late 30s and early 40s looking to take home young professionals or college students who obviously had too much to drink.

She was with two of her friends from work, and they were hanging on a group of guys. That was another new thing. I mean, her talking to guys wasn't new, but her and her friends hanging on them, acting drunk before they even got two drinks down, was.

She laughed at something one of the guys said, throwing her head back and then forward, where it landed near his chest. Her hand was on his arm. It was a muscular arm, the short sleeves of his shirt stretched like Joan Rivers' face. He was tall, had short blonde hair, khaki shorts, a tattoo on his lower calf, a big watch, an earring, and a chest that screamed "I love protein[12] and establishing new personal bench press records!" Pretty much everything I wasn't.

"Oh, hi Grey!" she exclaimed much too loudly. "Come here!" I pretty much had to if I wanted to talk to her, because she wasn't coming to me.

"How was work?" she asked, and then we were into it. Forced introductions, Julie every now and then throwing me into the middle of the conversation so I wouldn't "feel left out," though I'd much rather have only talked as a voluntary participant, where I could have eased in, made a well-timed quip or witty remark that may have actually earned little tidbits of respect from the crowd. Not that I wanted their respect. It would have been ideal if I could have elicited respect from them, then showed them how indifferent I was to it. Julie knew that about me, hated it and never understood it. I couldn't explain why I was that way, but, you know, that's why leopards have different spots, right? Or something like that.

The drive home wasn't any better, me in the passenger seat listening to the laughter and loudness of three intoxicated women. Even though I didn't even have two drinks, and Julie threw back four that I counted, she still drove. And it's not like she was drunk, or swerving all over the road, but I thought it would make sense if I drove, because I knew she'd want to talk to her friends about everybody. But it was Julie's car, and she couldn't have any of the seating presets changed or the rearview mirror touched. She had to drive. I knew this and didn't even ask.

We got home a little before two and went to bed. She went right to sleep and I stayed awake, lying on my back, looking at the ceiling, smelling her alcohol and Listerine breath.

Saturday meant Julie sleeping in. I woke at eight, showered and dressed in silence, and slipped out the front door on my way to Korner Koffee. This was routine—me waking first on weekends and fetching bagel sandwiches and coffee.

Let me clarify something here: I don't want you to get the impression that Julie was no good, and never did anything for me. It wasn't like that. She packed me lunches for work, though she rarely packed one for herself. And she did my laundry, and rubbed my head—to me, having my head rubbed was almost as enjoyable as getting my other head rubbed; well, not really almost, but it was a second—pumped me up in bed, and gave me confidence. But like I said, that was a story in itself, and that story occurred before this story. She wasn't a bad person—nothing like that. It was just obvious that our train was slowing down, too much friction on the track.

When I returned, she was in her pajamas on the sofa, smoking a cigarette and watching the local Saturday morning show on tv.

"What'd you get?"

"What'd I get? Bagel and egg sandwiches. Coffee. And good morning to you."

"Grab me some juice while you're in the kitchen," she said. "And a napkin. And a plate."

"Should I chew the food for you too?"

As we were eating, a hugely fat woman—Mo—was on location at a restaurant. The host of the show said, "Stay tuned, because in our Modern Marvel Makeover, Mo is going to surprise a waitress. You don't want to miss it."

"What's she gonna do, order a salad?" I asked offhandedly.

"What do you know about it?" Julie snapped. "Always making fun of people. What's so special about you?" And she had a point, sure, but the thing that took me back was that she always used to laugh at my jokes (especially the ones about other people—the ones about her, not so much). We used to sit in Rittenhouse Square and poke fun of anyone we could. Exaggerate quirks, point out hipsters. We'd laugh, and we'd enjoy ourselves. Julie getting annoyed at my jokes was one more example of how far we'd come from those early days.

"What? I'm just joking. Christ, what's your problem?"

"Nothing," she said, crumbling her napkin in a ball and throwing it on the table. "I'm taking a shower. I don't feel well."

Here we are.

Julie grew up in love with the idea of being a good wife. She didn't really care about much else, like where she lived or what kind of job she'd have. In fact, having "good wife" as her employment would have suited her just fine.

It was, as some may say, a romantic notion.

But then, through no fault of her own, she got selfish. She wanted things for herself. She became human. And wasn't she entitled to that? Weren't people more selfish nowadays anyway? Besides, there would be plenty of time to be a good wife when she was ready.

She didn't tell me this, and I didn't deduce this on a basis of her personality. I heard her on the phone one day. I was in the other room watching tv. When she was on the phone, she talked as if nobody around her could hear.

Not that she cared, obviously.

Was the fact that life was so complicated in the 21st Century a large reason for so many people being miserable? Should people go back to aspiring to be nothing more than good fathers, or wives, or family folk? When things were simpler? But I'm sure there were a lot of miserable people back then, too. So I guess I don't have much of a point.

* * *

Throughout this story, you'll notice that I write "Here we are" every so often. That's not a nervous tick or anything, but a Lamken saying. They say "Here we are" when they talk. It's like how we say, "Um," or "like." I dig it, because whatever you're doing, there you are.

Here we are.

* * *

As a young married couple, Jeff and Celia had a Saturday routine that worked for them. Celia woke first, early, took a morning shower. Earlier in the marriage, Jeff sometimes joined her, and they'd start the day off right. Now, Jeff brushed his teeth, getting his fuzzy view through the shower door, and went to the kitchen to start breakfast. He enjoyed cooking, and an evening watching the Good Network was good television. They'd have breakfast with the E network or reruns of American Idle[13].

Then, Jeff would head outside to start on some yard work, or look for something that might need fixing, anything to do with his hands. After a week in an office, working outdoors made him feel good. Besides, he preferred to stay home more often nowadays, since he was more regular with his bathroom visits than he would have liked.

On the Saturdays when Celia didn't work, shopping was a must, even if she didn't spend any money. The real pleasure lay in going store to store, walking among the crowds, drawing looks from men and teenage boys, fantasizing that she could buy whatever she wanted.

Sometimes she'd go into stores that, instead of having dressing rooms in the back, had little changing areas lined against the walls. These were basically closets with curtains. Many times, she'd change into sweaters or little t-shirts and leave the curtain a few inches open. And she'd notice men and teenage boys looking in, some basically salivating, and she'd let them gawk. Sometimes she'd take several different shirts in and change, sometimes she'd take her bra off, sometimes she'd pretend she was hosting an award show and kept coming out on stage in different outfits. But she never changed pants in any of those. She felt that would be trashy.

She changed pants in dressing rooms, and always kept the door shut.

* * *

And for a lot of people in the 20-30-year-old set without children, this was basically it. Work and the weekend. Although many people craved excitement, and did a lot to ward off impish boredom, they never really got anything to get excited about for more than an hour or so. For a lot of people, the anticipation of something good wasn't even enough.

Though there was a whole lot going on in the world that could have occupied time and prompted action, most people didn't concern themselves too much with that. I was certainly one of those people. There was a whole lot that I didn't necessarily agree with, but I couldn't let it bother me. See, I didn't live in the world. I lived in a duplex with Julie in Philadelphia.

Though not for long.

Chapter Four

Breaking Up Isn't So Hard to Do

A lot of time, you can find what you're looking for,
but usually only if you keep looking for it.
—Grey Reflections

I don't remember everything about the morning. A lot was a blur, mostly due to the fact that I was awfully hung-over. We both were, having had way too much to drink the night before, Julie swerving down the road as she drove and me not caring as much about safety as with getting home without throwing up in the car.

Looking back, I guess her kicking me out of the house was no big surprise.

The fact that it came on the heels of her tripping over my boots.... Well, I guess something had to trigger it, and that was as good a reason as any.

She yelled, I yelled back in a passive-aggressive kind of way, and though it could have been worse, it still was pretty messy. We both said some things that, later on, I'm sure we didn't mean. But like I said, the break-up wasn't too much of a shock to either of us. What was a shock was learning that Julie had been fucking both Carlos and Mrs. McCarthy, including a few sessions of both at the same time. That surprised me for about two and a half seconds.

After we got it all out of our systems and I started packing, she had the nerve to ask me if I was going to get breakfast. I told her I wasn't hungry. She offered to help me pack if I'd get her a bagel sandwich and coffee. I agreed, if only to not be around her. When I returned, all she'd done was put my laptop, a couple books, and a few CDs in a box, and balled some clothes into my laundry bag. She told me she couldn't find the rest of my things.

She ate her sandwich and drank her coffee while I gathered my stuff. Fortunately, there wasn't much.

She told me I could stay on the couch for as long as I needed, assuming it wasn't an unreasonable amount of time, like two weeks. But I didn't want to stay there. Again, I didn't hate her, and I know she didn't hate me. But our time was over, and we knew it.

* * *

"If you need somewhere to go," Jeff said, "crash at our place until you find something."

"I don't know," I said. "What about Celia? I don't want to cause any trouble."

"We have two extra bedrooms. Well, one is the computer room, but the other is empty. At least it'll be a roof over your head. Besides, you can ride to work with me. And don't worry about Celia. It's my house too, you know."

So for two weeks, I bunked at Jeff and Celia's. Like I said, I didn't have much, and slept on some blankets and pillows; but Jeff was right, it was a roof over my head and a ride to work. And having constant company somewhat softened the blow of the break-up. We watched television and talked at night. I know they enjoyed having me there as well, as they no longer depended on each other for conversation.

I think my temporary residence also helped Jeff and Celia's sex life, for Jeff was much more chipper in the mornings. And if that didn't tip me off, Celia's (what I can only guess were) exaggerated moans and shrieks—it sounded like she was getting exorcised; there was a lot of shit in languages I've never heard before—from the bedroom were enough of a clue.

The bedroom gymnastics didn't bother me. I'd put on my headphones and pretty much tune them out. Once—okay, a few times—I masturbated while they were going at it, but those instances were almost always assisted by laptop porn.

Living with Celia was interesting, to say the least. She'd wear revealing clothes around the house. No bras, tight sweatpants. And whenever she could bend down in front of me, she did. When parts of her came into my line of vision, she'd look to see if I was looking. If I was, she smiled. And I'm sure her making so much noise in the bedroom at night was because she now had an audience instead of just a partner.

"Did anyone ever tell you that you look like Al Pacino?" she asked one day.

"Uh, no, can't say anyone has."

"Well I think you could pass for him. You know, a younger version of him. A Serpico, without the beard. Either him or Alex P. Keaton."

"Michael J. Fox?"

"Yeah, but I'll always know him as Alex P. Keaton."

People were on a first-name basis with celebrities.

Another thing I noticed was that she watched reality shows with a bipolarity that was downright disturbing. She'd either be so into it, talking to characters and engaging in solo conversations with us about who was going to win, why they should win, and what they'll do after the show; or she'd be screaming at Jeff to change the channel, and saying that the girls were ugly or fat or stupid, and the judges were on drugs.

Jeff and I knew that her hostility was because of her Survivor-show near miss, and kept silent.

* * *

After two weeks of sharing a roof with them, Peppercorn came through.

"I think I got something for you," he said.

"What?"

"A place to live."

"Really? Where?"

"In Media[14]. First floor apartment. It's not that big, but it'll do you just fine. It's right by the train station, too, so you don't have to worry about getting a car."

I didn't bother asking how he found the place. I was sure it was owned by somebody he knew, and that was good enough for me.

I liked it. It was in an old insurance building. Small, but I didn't care. My world was shrinking, anyway.

I took a trip to IKEA with Jeff and picked up a couple of chairs and a futon. I had a 27-inch flat screen tv (and was pleasantly surprised when I plugged the cable wire into t.v. to find the feed on, thus providing free cable).

Media has a Main Street. It has little shops, unique restaurants, ice cream parlors, health food stores and coffee shops. There's the Media Theater. I never went to a show. I never glanced up at the marquee, never even knew what was playing. I didn't care.

I got a kitten from the SPCA so I wouldn't be so lonely.

I named her Althea.

It worked.

Part II

Chapter Five

Decisions and Lamkens

He was a mythic figure, a marble statue of a Greek god come to life.
—S.T. Youvie, from his book, "The Real S.T.,"
referring to Dylan Maderwood V

Dylan Maderwood V was the man. A Decision Maker. Powerful.

Maderwood V was unapologetic in everything he did. He knew that he and his colleagues had a duty to supply the American public with what was best for them, in making for them the all-important Decisions they could not and should not be allowed to make. His crusade was one that saved American lives daily.

He also knew that with great wealth and great power came great responsibility. Whenthe Decision Makers Decided something, that was it. They couldn't listen to critics, instead using as their credo the Jonathan Swift quote: "When a true genius appears, you can know him by this sign: that all the dunces are in a confederacy against him."

Maderwood V stood 6'6", weighed 285 pounds, had immense hands that swallowed up those they shook. Sandy brown hair that stood petrified in neat little rows running from his fingertips, up his arms, to his chest, back, head, down to his feet, though it skipped his legs. He followed in the footsteps of his grandfather and father, Dylan Maderwood III and Dylan Maderwood IV, as energy mavens. He was a modern man's Prometheus, harnessing oil and electricity to dispense it to the masses, for fees they'd surely pay.

He was a Harvard man. Or was it a Yale man? I never could remember which. Not that it mattered.

Maderwood V did not have military experience. None of the Decision Makers did. Another thing they had in common was each had a III or IV or Jr. or Sr. after his name. There were no black, Asian, Latino, or (God forbid) Native American Decision Makers. That would only complicate things.

What Maderwood V did have was an uncanny ability to predict the future—and more importantly, how he and his colleagues could benefit from those predictions. For example, it was Maderwood V's stroke of absolute genius[15] that swelled the proliferation of credit and debit cards as the preferred—and oftentimes only—method of payment. As a result, cash was placed on the endangered species list.

But thanks to the Lamkens, cash will never become extinct.

Maderwood V also knew that raising credit limits for people would make them spend more. And the more they spent, the more they owed. And the more they owed, the more they paid in interest.

"In its simplest form," he said, "economics is really a beautiful science."

And the more people owed, the more likely they would meet the banks' girlfriend, Ms. Penalty Fee, and her fraternal twin, Mr. Late Payment.

Maderwood V's ultimate idea was having credit card companies—which were owned by the banks—which were majority-owned by Decision Makers—convince people with huge debt to pay off what they owed with the equity of their homes, which they didn't own but were in huge debt to the banks for. Once they did that, they were paying huge bills with high rates to people who, legally, could take their homes.

After all, real estate is the best market to corner.

* * *

There were five Decision Makers, and whenever they wanted to discuss business, to get down to brass tacks, they'd meet in an ultra-secret place in an undisclosed location. As a matter of fact, I write not far from it.

Privacy was integral for the Decision-Making process, and the United States had become too curious about everything in the past 30 years. Everybody wanted everything out in the open, and there were cameras and microphones and computers everywhere.

So about 20 years before this story, it was Decided that a new operational headquarters was needed, outside the continental U.S. They found a small island in the Pacific, about 1,000 miles from Hawaii. The island, Lamken, was about twice the size of Oahu, and was unknown to the rest of the world.

The secrecy of the Decision Makers' meeting place was of the utmost importance, so they instilled a security about the place that made Area 51 look like an open barn with no farmer in sight. A no-fly and no-sail zone was implemented 100 miles around the perimeter, and the island wasn't acknowledged on any map or on Google Earth. Satellite pictures were blocked out by an electronic device that made fuzzy snow on anything that attempted to photograph it.

Even though there were people on Lamken when the Decision Makers arrived, it wasn't difficult for them to take it over in the name of American interest. They assured the natives that space would be set aside and used for Decisions to be made. The natives offered no resistance, and conveyed to the Decision Makers that they were a peaceful people. What they did not convey, or what the Decision Makers never grasped, was that they also were very clever. In fact, it was their cleverness that made them what they are today.

As it happened, the Decision Makers—the men in suits—began meeting on Lamken shortly after Los and Mas climbed Mount Laddis. That was, of course, when Los was shown the vision of New Utopia. When the Decision Makers landed, the natives—led by Los—showed no emotion. Lamken legend has it that as soon as Los saw Mas astride the winged horse, he knew the prophecy would come true. So nobody was surprised when the first part of the vision was fulfilled.

Of course, Los wasn't the first person with a utopian vision, and I'm sure he won't be the last. But he was one of the few who saw it happen.

The Decision Makers' forefathers also experienced visions of a Utopia, some 500 years before. They saw a land teeming with resources, where they could live in peace and raise their families without kings and queens, where people could govern themselves. Once they found the land, the hard part was over. They didn't let anything stand in their way, running over forest and people and animal in building their Utopia.

The Decision Makers constructed a hastily-built but elegant meeting space. The Decision Makers even allowed the Lamkens to lend a hand. They viewed the Lamkens as pets, and were thrilled to learn how easily they picked up English. This made it so much easier for the Decision Makers to tell them what to do.

Along with Maderwood V, Decision Makers included Dennis Mathey III, great-great-grandson of a 5,000-acre cotton plantation owner and current president and majority stockholder in Mathey's Materials, the largest clothing shipping industry in the Western Hemisphere; David Morsty IV, great-grandson of a steel giant who had worked closely with Henry Ford, and the railroads before that; Morsty cursed like a sailor, though he always got seasick whenever he stepped foot on a boat; Donald Menginth IX, whose ancestors were among the first Europeans to land in America; and Duncan Manow, who recently joined the circle after replacing his brother, Daniel Manow VI, the victim of a fatal heart attack when trying to swim in his indoor pool far too quickly after having eaten lunch, which was between the legs of his 23-year old female assistant.

Although Menginth IX had seniority as the oldest (and the one with the highest number after his name), Maderwood V was the unquestioned leader. And powerful people have right-hand men. Dylan's was his son-in-law, S.T. Youvie.

S.T. was picked on as a child. It wasn't anything worse than what kids do to unpopular classmates, but we know that kids can be quite cruel. One of the nicknames they called him was S.T.D., which morphed into Herpes and AIDS and gonnor-eeeee-ah and siph-I-lusss. To combat the teasing, S.T. lifted weights, but never got any bigger. He was between 5'6" and 5'8", depending on what shoe he wore, and he had premature white hair. He also bore a scar from the edge of his right eyelid that slid into his hairline, the consequence of his tumbling over a barbed-wire fence when he was seven years old and getting chased by a Labrador retriever that he thought was foaming at the mouth. The whiteness around the dog's jaws was only Cool Whip, and the sugar made him chase after S.T. in a playful way.

S.T. clawed his way into an Ivy League university, where he had nothing but disdain for athletes and foreign students. After a socially uneventful three years, he met a young woman outside of a professor's office during his final semester. It wasn't a surprise for the two to meet there—the woman was involved in an affair with the professor, and S.T. spent more time with teachers than students, claiming that professors were the only ones on a mental par with him.

In actuality, much hadn't changed from grade school—students didn't want to hang with S.T. at all. For that matter, neither did professors, who called him names like Herpes and gonnor-eeeee-ah and siph-I-luss behind his back.

The young woman, Rose, stumbled right into his arms as she spilled out of the professor's office. She was in tears, and buried her head into S.T. simply because he was there. Not knowing how to react, S.T. stroked the back of her head and said nothing, smelling her strawberry shampoo and wondering what could be more wonderful than a woman's shampooed and conditioned head. He knew Rose attended his school, but didn't know it was her head buried in his chest. She was the closest thing to a damsel in distress he'd ever met.

What caused the end of Rose's affair with the professor was that she had an unpleasant odor emanating from her vagina, which gynecologists couldn't figure out, since she was very clean and washed herself at least twice a day. What made her problem even more vexing was that she could only reach orgasm through oral sex, but because of the odor, didn't find many willing partners.

S.T. never had a problem with that, because he hadn't smelled any other women and didn't know that Rose's cherry was rotten.

But what really made Rose smell like a fresh tulip to S.T. was her father.

S.T. knew all about the Maderwood energy empire and how the family hobnobbed with celebrities and politicians, the line between which grew muddier by the day.

Once S.T. and Rose were an item, suck up to Maderwood V S.T. did. And eventually S.T.'s sucking up paid off, as he was awarded the position of Undersecretary in the Northeast Department of Energy Security. S.T. was not a Decision Maker, but his position did wield power, and he was told by Maderwood V to make sure the people beneath him knew he had such power: "Power is something that people don't always know when they see. So remind them—at times subtly, at other times overtly. The more power people know you have over them, the more power they will cede to you."

After S.T. had his job, his power, and his place in a royal family, everything tasted and smelled good.

* * *

Some time between when I first left America and sat down to write this story, Youvie published his memoirs. The book promised that the author "left nothing out." It was a thin book, but did not receive much attention; surprising, since people like to read about another's fall from grace—and the harder the fall, the more engaging the story.

So S.T. must have fallen not only from grace, but from the minds of the American people. Maybe the main reason he flittered out of the memories of most Americans is because distractions kept getting better and better, more missiles being fired at the public on a second-to-second basis.

If you walked down the street now and asked 10 people what they thought about S.T. Youvie, I'd bet you the ones that could even identify him would say, "Him? He's old news!"

I bought his book for $24.95, though I'm sure you can get it for about 75 cents at a community book sale or online.

It's true what they say about online shopping—you can really get some good deals!

* * *

Do you want to know how wealthy the Decision Makers were? They had more money than many countries. They had more money than 90 percent of Americans would have if they lived to be 500 years old, and could work that long. They not only had more money than Americans—I wouldn't be surprised if they had more money than Americas! Central and South, of course.

The Decision Makers for years had known how valuable the ground was—and specifically, what was under it. So they dug deep, large holes. When those holes dried up, they dug new holes. Then they went into oceans. They damaged infrastructure by drilling so many holes everywhere in the earth, but that was mere collateral damage that couldn't be avoided. Their machinery was giant termites gorging on a wooden planet, turning everything to dust.

The Decision Makers didn't scam as much as brilliantly rely on people's apathy, selfishness, impotence, and ability to be distracted and unmotivated.

They were, deep down, surprised that so many possessed such qualities.

But their main weapon was their bankroll. They had the funds to beat the house, and they made it look so easy.

After energy and real estate, the next best thing was loansharking.

The Decision Makers held with long fingers some part of the businesses that loaned millions of dollars to millions of people each day, from five dollar trips to the grocery store to cars to houses. They charged anywhere from four to more than 100 percent interest. And those who welch didn't get their legs broken.

Much worse.

They got their balls broken; and if that didn't do the trick, they'd have their spirits snapped next. The Decision Makers had a countless number of people in their pockets, Mafia dons on an immense, impersonal scale.

The country had, for years, been sectioning into two socio-economic halves—those with a whole lot of money, and those with hardly any. Logically, the main goal of those with a whole lot was to make sure those with hardly any didn't get their hands on too much.

When I was a kid, there wasn't so large of a gap between those with a whole lot and those with hardly any. In fact, most people weren't in either category. The majority had enough money; their class was in the middle of the other two. They owned homes and cars, always had food, sent their kids to decent-enough schools, and, mostly, were fine.

Then—and this by no means started the genocide of the middle class, but it's when I took notice—many many people started losing their homes. The banks and companies who had lent the middle class money for the homes jacked up interest rates to a vig that was far too high.

The Decision Makers didn't run for office. Why should they? They weren't in the business of risking defeats, of having their lives all over the world's stage, of obligations. Most importantly, they weren't about to have their Decisions second- and third- and fourth-guessed. They were much happier to conduct their work in covert locations, away from the interruption of everyday life.

Dylan once told me that it was much easier having to stay in power for 10 or 20 years than having to be elected every two or four years. "How would anything get done?" he asked. "You'd spend half of your time working on getting elected, and the other half bickering with the other side. We, on the other hand, get things done. In fact, the terms of senators and congressmen are nothing more than two-year filibusters."

When he wanted to, Dylan could be quite poetic.

—From "The Real S.T."

I know you might be thinking that the Decision Makers couldn't have held power like the Supreme Court, or the president. But guess what? Somebody has to sign the checks for those people, too.

Each Decision Maker was assigned a quadrant of the country: Maderwood V had the Northeast, from D.C. to Maine. Each Decision Maker had an undersecretary in a security field[16], though S.T. was the only one who took his job seriously. The others simply wanted to cash paychecks and lead lives of luxury—which, after all, was entitled them by the Constitution.

Chapter Six

Americans in America

If they don't have a pill for it, you must really be fucked up.
—Grey Reflections

Not that they didn't before, but people's minds in America at this time whirred like appliances, on an on, so fast they couldn't always stop to grab hold of anything. Some spun so quickly they couldn't tell that they even whirred at all.

This concept is analogous to the concept that Earth spins so fast, nothing on the planet knows it is spinning. But if it stopped, even for a second, gravity would have a field day.

Since people's brains whirred like appliances, pharmaceutical companies were Maytag men. But unlike Maytag men, who waited and waited for something to fix, drug companies were quite busy. They could temporarily alter the whirring of an individual's appliance, though the changes were usually unknown and not necessarily for the better.

Mind-numbing, anti-anxiety pills such as Valium and Xanax sold in large numbers, and my generation's preferred soother, Santonium, sold so quickly that doctors couldn't write prescriptions fast enough. Some doctors took it to combat the stresses of writing so many prescriptions. When even Dubs Security Systems couldn't provide comfort and shield people from the dangers, stress, and new season of "Taste of Lovin,"[17] Santonium could. It wrapped its warm self around troubled minds and rocked people to an endorphin-flooded serenity.

Drug companies wanted to address anything and everything a person could suffer from. There were pills if you were anxious, nervous, depressed, had an achy back, fear of flying, fear of crashing, if you laughed to much, didn't laugh at all, tanned too easily, couldn't tan at all, couldn't get an erection, came too soon, didn't come fast enough, couldn't make a left turn during rush-hour, or couldn't decide on which pill to take for which ailment.

* * *

One—but not certainly the sole—reason for so many anti-anxiety medicines was the price of gasoline, which rose slowly but steadily, like the erection of a dirty old man at a junior high school graduation.

I remember when I was a teenager, driving around with Loo P, the first one of us old enough to drive, in his brother's Monte Carlo. Five or six kids from the neighborhood would pile in and prowl the streets, just to see who was out.

We'd ante up gas money. By that, I mean that four of us would buck up about one dollar apiece. And we'd get more than a quarter tank of gas, enough to keep us driving around for the day.

At this time, if people wanted to fill their gas tanks up, they might've needed either a 50 or 100 dollar bill—sometimes both!

Not surprisingly, entrepreneurial robbers figured that if everybody needed to put 50 or 100 dollars worth of fuel in their car, gas stations would have a lot of 50 and 100 dollar bills in their registers. Why not rob gas stations? they asked themselves. They could even fill up while they were there!

The only problem for the entrepreneurial robbers was that, if you recall your history lesson from a few pages back, many many people in America didn't use dollar bills anymore. They used the plastic cards that Maderwood V so brilliantly pushed to soften the blow of spending money. If people paid for things with plastic instead of paper, they might not realize how much they spent. And with interest, people usually wound up paying more than what things cost, just for that momentary piece of mind of not having to fork over dollar bills.

It's like that old gambling saying Peppercorn once told me: "The guy who invented casinos was smart, but the guy who invented chips was a genius."

Sometimes, when robbers were told that there wasn't nearly as much money in the register as they suspected there'd be, they'd get mad, and scared, and do things like pull triggers.

So gas stations needed to do something to combat this. Owners figured that, if they had guns of their own, they could even the playing field. And if a clerk shot a robber, it would not only give that particular gas station great publicity on the news—it might even wind up on COPS!—it would be the best deterrent for future robbers.

So people who had extremely vested interests in gas stations lobbied for lawmakers to write a measure that would allow clerks to carry concealed or non-concealed weapons at Sunoco A-Pluses, Gettys, Exxon-Mobils, BPs, and B & J Bushes. The bill passed quicker than shit through a goose. Bang bang.

Many gas station owners in the South just chuckled and wondered what the hell took so long for the rest of the country to wise up and do what they'd been doing for decades.

* * *

To the Decision Makers, energy crises did not exist. In fact, no crisis existed. That word, to them, could have been struck from the dictionary and they wouldn't have skipped a beat.

Some causes for high gas prices: Fog. No fog. Unseasonably cold winters. Unseasonably warm winters. Hurricanes. Tornados. Wind, but not the kind that you could use for energy. Beavers building a dam near a refinery. Birds and other wildlife using spilled oil as a fashion statement. Survival of species.

* * *

Philadelphia Daily News, June 3

Shootout at gas station leaves three shot; two dead

Two men were shot and killed and one injured late last night during an attempted robbery at a Sunoco gas station in Springfield, Delaware County. This is the first incident of gas station violence to hit the Philadelphia region, following a

> trend of similar attacks already seen in other parts of the country.
>
> Shortly before midnight, Dan DeLucia, night manager at the Sunoco A-Plus on Baltimore Pike and Prince Avenue, shot at the robbers in self defense, using his registered Tech-9 semi-automatic pistol. The robbers wanted money, but got lead instead.

I witnessed this shootout. I was pulling into the station when a car screeched to a stop. One man got out and rushed to the little window booth, pulling a gun. That's all I needed to see, and I got the hell out of there. Before I got out, I heard several little pops, not nearly as loud as what I thought a gun sounded[18]. I never turned back. As soon as I got home, I turned on the tv and called Jeff.

"Dude, you won't believe what just happened!"

"Wait a second!" he said. "Turn on the news! There was a shootout in Springfield!"

"I know, at a gas station! I was there."

I heard Celia in the background screaming at the tv, asking how they could let the reporter wear something that did nothing for her figure.

I watched the news for hours, gorging myself on extended coverage. I called Pepper to tell him about it, but he was playing poker at the casino and could not possibly have cared less. A little after midnight, though, I got a call from another inquiring mind.

"Do you believe this?" Julie asked.

"Yeah," I said. "Crazy." I knew that I shouldn't have answered the phone, but I did.

"This *is* crazy! Isn't that near where you live now?"

"Yeah. I actually was there when it—"

"You know, I miss having you with me when something like this happens. I miss talking to you about it."

"I miss you too. I miss—"

Through the phone, I heard Julie's doorbell ring.

"Hold on a sec."

I heard a muffled man's voice.

"Okay, let me go. I'll talk to you later."

She hung up.

Thank god I had continuing coverage all night long of the shootout to help me pass the time. I hardly thought about her at all.

* * *

Even with these economic problems, America still was the richest country in the world, and danced so well to find ways to magically avoid two losing quarters, since it hated wearing the crown of recession. For a lot of people, the economy was doing just fine. Unfortunately, I wasn't one of them. In fact, I was about to be fired from my job.

In the four years I'd worked at PIMBCO, we'd hear once a year how profits weren't as high as expected, or that the company was facing a merger, or that there may be downsizing. The first couple of times, I'd been understandably fearful of joining the swelling ranks of the unemployed. Jeff, though, would reassure me that this stuff happened, and the only ones ever let go were menial workers whose positions could quickly be rehired with cheaper labor, or divvied among other workers. Since my job was full-time, and the work really couldn't be heaped upon another employee, I had nothing to worry about. And it must have been true, because I kept a job for four years, even though I did nothing above and beyond my job description to necessarily warrant one.

A while back, in the 1980s, the term "trickle-down economics" became popular. I never understood what it meant; I had to look it up on Google. It was an economic philosophy that argued that if businesses and corporations flourish, their revenue and net economic gains would trickle down to benefit even the poorest of people. The theory is much more involved than that, of course. While I was looking it up, I came across a saying by the economist John Kenneth Galbraith, whom I'd never heard of before and whose name I most likely will never mention again unless I'm watching Jeopardy. The saying was, "If you feed enough oats to a horse, some will pass through to the road for the sparrows."

This saying summed up not only trickle-down economics, but also the entire philosophy of the Decision Makers. The rich and powerful eat eat eat, and the rest of us get to pick through their shit for anything that might be salvageable.

I—along with almost 20 percent of the workforce—was fired. Turns out PIMBCO must not have been too concerned with facts, after all.

Here we are.

Chapter Seven

Lamkens in America

Sometimes, even Decision Makers have things Decided for them by the little head.

—Grey Reflections

In the 1970s, four Decision Makers became understandably enraptured with the beauty of Lamken women. With caramel skin, full lips, almond eyes, straight black hair, and a sense of servitude, Lamken women were everything the Decision Makers could have dreamed. Seeing that Lamken had no money and little else, they used their entrepreneurial know-how to design a win-win situation: In what they deemed a price far above market value, they offered 40,000 dollars for four young women. They explained to the Lamkens that with this money, the islanders could buy—from the Decision Makers—food, material for sturdy homes, and the most important thing, luxuries. The only thing they did not know was how the Lamkens would respond to an offer for their people.

Due to Los' vision, the Decision Makers' request was not met with scorn. After a tribal consultation, the chief elder, Wischa, replied he did not want 10,000 dollars apiece. He wanted a machine that would enable the Lamkens to print their own money. The Decision Makers laughed and applauded Lamken ingenuity, and said no problem. They flew to the island a money-printing machine, had a Classified Service agent give a quick demonstration on how it worked, and provided all the materials necessary for the Lamkens to print as much money as they wanted.

The Lamkens got to work. In fact, that's all they did for many many years. They printed money 24 hours a day, and distributed it to their people. They printed American dollars and created their own currency. They didn't want to rank Elders by value, have someone placed on the one and someone on the hundred and someone on the thousand, so they put the sun on the one, the moon on the five, a coconut on the ten, an ocean on the twenty, a silhouette of a voluptuous woman on the fifty, a totem pole on the hundred, and an eagle on the thousand.

And with all this currency, their own and American, they bought bought bought from the Decision Makers. They even requested that they be allowed to trade and buy items on the world market, which they had heard about in the Decision Maker meetings. The Decision Makers didn't like that last idea, since the Lamkens joining the world market would bring attention, something the Decision Makers didn't want imported to Lamken. So the Decision Makers gave the Lamkens huge catalogues with everything you could imagine to browse through, and the Lamkens paid cash for everything and anything.

If any of the Lamkens didn't have enough money for a particular item, the Elders made more for that person.

* * *

Although the four women who captivated the Decision Makers didn't want to leave their homes, they did not refuse. The Elders assured them they were chosen ones, and carried a great deal of responsibility. The women were to service, in any way, these older, white men, and learn as much as they could about American life, culture, and customs. They were to report this information to the Elders through letters and correspondence. To keep the information secret, they wrote in their Lamken language, which I still cannot read or write. When spoken, it is very rhythmic, and reminds me of hip-hop.

All of the correspondence is in the Lamken library, and has been translated into English, Spanish, French, Italian, and Chinese. The Lamkens did that will all their canonical works.

This book has not been translated.

As shown by their ability to so easily grasp English, Lamkens are uncanny at learning any language they hear, no matter how old they are when first exposed to it. They are the only known humans to possess such a skill. Linguists would think they died and went to heaven if they could study these people for a year.

And it isn't just human languages that Lamkens pick up so easily. One cannot distinguish their bird cries from actual birds—not even the birds! *Ma-caw! Ma-caw!*

It goes without saying that Lamkens also mastered the financial and political languages, in which so many people around the world cope with illiteracy.

I've never seen one, but I swear I hear whales, especially at night. Of course, it could just be some mischievous Lamken adolescent, having fun with his Zelig voice.

I refuse to believe that. I want to see a whale.

* * *

The Decision Makers brought their young, exotic mistresses to America and Decided not to separate them. The women were set up in four small, furnished homes on the edge of the Philadelphia Main Line. This ensured that the mistresses would be far enough away from the Decision Makers' real homes, but close enough for a quick layover whenever the Decision Makers were in the neighborhood and in the mood. Within two years, four American-Lamken children were born—three boys and one girl.

The Decision Makers who fathered the half-Lamken children never paid them any attention—they just paid for them. They gave the Lamken women and their children a good enough salary each month and made sure all of their bills were taken care of. The only requisite was that the women or children could never say who the real fathers were, could never say anything about who they were or who they knew. This was for their own good, for the Decision Makers informed them that nobody would believe them, and the women knew this to be true. Besides, the women and children could suddenly disappear, and nobody would know, or care. The women knew this to be true as well.

Veiled threats and warnings aside, the Decision Makers weren't necessarily mean to their half-families. They even offered to send the women and children back to Lamken, as the Decision Makers had lost interest sexually in the women after the babies were born. But they chose to stay, and the Decision Makers didn't blame them, saying, "Why would they want to go back? They never knew how good life could be."

The women loved tending their gardens. They knitted and watched tv. The children were home-schooled and read everything they could.

The women sent letters to the Elders once a week, and received a letter once a week in return from the Elders. They did this until email allowed them to communicate more frequently and with greater grammatical errors. The children learned of their island's history electronically—a little different than hearing it around a fire by storytellers who animate characters next to you, but not too much. When they turned 16, they were told of Los' vision, and what Lamken was to become. They heard of the crucial role they'd possibly play in Lamken's Utopian formation. What that role would be was not clear at the time—but they were to prepare themselves for the moment, should it come.

They accepted this news with reverence. The Lamkenfest Destiny, if you will.

I don't know how American children would react to hearing news like this on their 16th birthday. I guess some would react better than others. It depended on who heard the news, and if they had anything better to do that night.

One other thing about the Decision Makers who impregnated the achingly beautiful, caramel-skinned, innocent young women of Lamken: They had never seen their half-Lamken children. Not even a picture.

Chapter Eight

Lamkens in Lamken

We must not delay, nor must we act in haste.
—Wischa

When the search party found Los after the 12th day, he had aged dramatically, with large circles under his eyes and his once-black hair completely white. He told his vision repeatedly, and it soon became the creed of the Lamkens, giving them the one thing they had wanted from the ascension of Mount Laddis—hope.

Around the time the Decision Makers first met on the island and introduced technology to the Lamkens—fulfilling the first part of Los' prophecy—the Elders unanimously elected to Chief Elder Los' son Les, who at this time was in his sixth decade. He served in this role for less than five years, his life shortening out when a school of electric eels, or knifefish, decided to leave their home waters off the coast of South America and start over as, I guess, big fish in a smaller pond. But they weren't prepared to travel as long as they did, and when they got to the shores of Lamken, they were so distraught and frustrated that they took it out on everything they saw: other fish, low-flying birds, and Les, who was out for a midnight swim.

His body was never found, even though the Lamkens searched the waters for months. Not a trace of bone or flesh or organ was found. It was as if Les' body and spirit just morphed into the water.

The knifefish were never heard from again, either; I guess they didn't make it big.

After Les' death, the Lamkens turned to his son, Los' grandson, Wischa. And though Wischa was only in his fourth decade, and no more than 35 years old, he was named Chief Elder.

Wischa was inducted in an elaborate ceremony, with dancing and food and fire and sex. His first edict was for Lamken to have an official story, which was to begin with his grandfather's vision.

So one was written. It was the first Lamken book. I don't know who wrote it.

You know what they called it? Ourstory.

Not history.

Aren't foreigners funny?

Here we are.

The Lamken library is stocked with all sorts of books. Classics and fiction and non-fictions, most of which they've imported. There is a large section of Lamken authors, because all any Lamken has to do in order to publish a book is write one. The books Lamkens write are mostly about the island, or about native wildlife, or about their likes and dislikes. There's no guarantee that anyone will read it, but they don't seem to care.

The book you're holding is available at the Lamken library. I used to go there every day to see if anyone was reading it, but that got boring.

The Lamkens maintained a society based on respecting their lawmakers, the Elders. Even though women cannot be Lamken Elders[19], it is their vote that chooses new Elders.

The only election to draw complaints was when Long Dong, who was slow in mental capacity, was overwhelmingly named an Elder when at 19 years old. Every single woman—and some married ones—submitted his name on a write-in vote. The Elders in charge of the voting process vetoed the election; when that resulted in a backlash from Lamken women, Long Dong was made Elder Gigolo of the island, a position nobody but he had a problem with, since he always complained of being tired.

Wischa told him, "With greatness comes great responsibility."

Though they had never seen a map until the later 20th century, Lamken had a flag, gold and purple, regal colors if colors could be regal, with a white coconut moon in the upper left corner.

Lamkens had for as long as they lived on the island made houses and structures out of wood and an incredibly sturdy mud brick. Before the Decision Makers came, they subsided mostly on fish and fruit. You should see what they can do with shrimp, shellfish, sea urchin and tuna, and the variety of fruit is incredible. I don't know how all these different kinds of fruit can be found in one location. Plantains and papayas and pineapples and pears and plums and peaches and pomegranates and that's only the p's!

Now, they have feasts that put the ish in lavish. They even have their own vineyard, to make champagne and wine.

Breakfast is amazing. They've bought ovens in which to bake bread.

And Lamken has a proud contingent of the very birds that brought down the plane carrying Celia and 11 other Survivor contestants—plus crew, pilots and flight attendants. What kinds of birds? Finches, I know that. And herons and parrots and macaws, of course. And a bunch of others that I don't know. But the Lamkens don't hunt them, and the birds have remained unafraid of humans.

They have mountains, and wonderful fresh water lakes, and natural hot springs, and gorgeous weather. They are fortunate enough to be out of the way of hurricanes and monsoons, as if even nature doesn't wish to bother them.

Lamkens are color blind, and upon first encountering the white man, they only impressions the Decision Makers made on them were height and dress. All of the Decision Makers wore suits—except for Maderwood V, who never wore a tie—as did the Classified Service agents and pilots. The Lamkens didn't think much of pilots' uniforms—except for the helmets, which they absolutely loved.

Lamkens for years delivered prayers to the mouth of Mount Laddis. I don't know how high it is, footage-wise, but there's snow on its nipple. It splits the clouds, which don't seem to mind at all. In fact, it looks as if Mount Laddis and the clouds have a very healthy relationship.

Around Lamken runs a wonderful ring of coral, every color. If you climb to one of the lookout points and gaze a few miles out, it's like a kaleidoscope, the sun shining off of shells and rocks, reflected through the water's clarity.

If anyone would have looked on Google Earth at where Lamken was before this story, he or she would only have seen pixilated images, so there was no proof of its existence.

If anyone would look on Google Earth at where Lamken is now, they'd see us tucked away somewhere between California and Australia.

I don't know the exact size of Lamken. There's no record of footage or anything. I've tried walking around it, but I kept getting distracted and would lose count after a couple hundred thousand steps.

Lamken has a national anthem, with words and bird and animal calls. When translated into English, the only words I can understand are, "Here we are," and "There we go," and "There we were," and "Yes we know."

Just as Mas predicted, the more the Decision Makers introduced to the Lamkens, the more the natives adapted. They quickly and inconceivably learned to harness the powers of electricity and hydropower. The Decision Makers found the Lamkens amusing and patted their heads for their advancements.

The Decision Makers did not think twice about the submission of the Lamkens, and allowed them to host with servitude.

The Lamkens watched, listened. It didn't take long to gather from these men in suits, these men who were unknowingly showing them their new way of life, that money is the key to happiness, and people with the most are the happiest. The Lamkens surmised, then, that if an entire population had all the money they wanted, an entire population would be happy.

This simple deduction was how Lamken became New Utopia.

Part III

Chapter Nine

Gotta Get Back on the Horse

You gotta take a shot—no risk, no reward.
—Peppercorn

I had, in a few weeks, lost my relationship, place to live, and job. Peppercorn found me a new place to live, and he came through again, with a job.

"Come work with me," he said. "Install security systems. It's so easy—people always want more security."

"I don't know anything about installing security systems," I said.

"So what? We'll be working together. We always made a great team. Remember in grade school, when we sold cupcakes that all of the mothers made for the class trip? We sold more than any class ever did."

"Yeah, but we pocketed half of the money for ourselves!" I said.

"We still sold more than anyone else. And the class went to Hershey Park, didn't we?"

"You don't do that now, do you?"

"What, go to Hershey Park?" he asked, smiling.

"No; you know, pocket, uh, extra commission?"

"Nah," Peppercorn said. "It's not worth it. Besides, I'm telling you, I'm doing fine on the legit side with this. I mean, I still have a few, you know, venture capital things; but I'm not skimming from Dubs. Even though I could be, believe me. He's about as sharp as a bag of wet hair."

"How do you know Dubs will even hire me?"

"Don't worry about it. It'll be no problem. He'll be happy to bring you aboard."

"I'd be happy to bring you aboard," Dubs said.

A couple of years before, Dubs got his start-up money the good ol' fashioned American way—he hit for half a million on a slot machine.

"You believe that?" Peppercorn once said. "That wouldn't happen to me in a thousand years. If it did, I'd get hit by a truck on my way out of the casino. Guy must sleep with angels, save nuns or something."

"Yeah," I said. "That's life-changing money."

"Depends on the life."

So less than a week after I was fired as a fact-checker, I was officially a security systems installer. And Peppercorn was right—the job was cake. The more secure people's homes were, the more security they needed.

Installing the systems was not nearly as complicated as one might think. It was all based on sensors that threw an invisible shield around the perimeter of whatever was being protected. An alarm sounded if the forcefield was broken, or if somebody entered the "forbidden zone," an automated dialer called the police or mafia or anyone else the system's owner wanted to notify. Sensors could snap pictures of intruders.

* * *

The gas crisis was having noticeable effects. Oil tanker jackings. Cars starving on the sides of roads, out of fuel. Siphonings. And worse.

"Have you heard the news?" Dubs said to me as I walked in the office one morning for my lineup of jobs for the day.

"Not yet."

"Check this out," he said, handing me the *Daily News*. He was giddy, and hopped back and forth from one foot to the other.

Philadelphia Daily News, June 19

Gas Station Bombs Pump South Philly

Reflecting the disturbing trend seen at gas stations around the country, a Sunoco station in South Philadelphia near Citizen's Bank Park was the latest to fall victim to an attack. Shortly after midnight, Dean Patrick's BP gas station was rocked with three loud explosions, toppling six pumps and destroying the parking lot. Authorities have no leads, yet believe the explosions were made with quarter sticks of dynamite.

With gasoline having been made a national preserve, the perpetrators can be charged with terroristic activities, meaning their punishment could land them chained to a rock on Cuba while large birds peck at their livers.

There was more to the story, but Dubs snatched the paper out of my hand.

"Can you believe this?" he asked.

"Yeah," I said. "Things are getting out of hand."

"Are you crazy?" he said. "This is the greatest thing in the world. We've already gotten calls from six Sunocos, three Texacos, eight Exxons, and a couple BPs. They all want security. Cameras installed around the pumps. I don't have to remind you of the money that gas stations have. This is too good to be true. I don't want to jinx it."

"Well, that's putting a positive spin on it."

"I want you to hit as many of the stations as possible today. I want you to push the deluxe camera line on all of them. Take the paper with you. Show them the story, even if they've read it. This is so great. So great."

Dubs provided me with a company car, a compact Geo Prism. I'd driven bigger bumper cars.

"Hi, I'm Grey, from Dubs Security," I said to the owner when I pulled into Dean's BP. It was decimated. Craters in the ground, sawhorses, yellow police tape. The whole place stunk; each inhalation was like being in a confessional with an Iranian cab driver off a 12-hour shift." Here to fix what ails you."

"Yeah, good to meet you," Dean said, with a little less than love. The butt of a shiny silver pistol proudly protruded from his waistband. He had a button-down denim shirt that was opened to his chest; a tattoo of Yosemite Sam holding two revolvers peeked out.

"Man, they really did a number on this place," I said.

"Yep. You fucking believe this? Had this place for almost 20 years; never even had an egg thrown at it. Now this."

"I'm sorry."

"Yeah. I'm just sorry I didn't catch them doing it."

"So, I hear you want full service," I said, trying a joke.

"You god-damn-a right," Dean said. "I want to be able to see everything from every angle of this station."

I installed cameras all over the gas station—by the front door, on top of each of the pumps, at ground level, and eye level, from the roof of the A-Plus. Though a monkey[20] could have done it, I made it seem much harder than it actually was, grimacing at times, scratching my head as if to figure out the best place to affix it, and measuring things that had nothing to do with installing security cameras.

"Is there a way you can hook these up so that I can watch from home?" Dean asked.

"Sure, not a problem. We even have universal remotes that work with almost every cable system. Just make sure you don't have anything in the microwave when you change the channel, because sometimes the 'enter' key on the remote changes microwave settings to high."

* * *

Then Peppercorn set me up with a castrator.

He said I was depressed. I said I wasn't. I said I didn't want a woman in my life right now. I let him convince me that having one in my life wasn't a bad idea.

"So who is this girl?"

"Oh, she's great," he said. "You'll love her."

"What does she look like?"

"Oh, that's too arbitrary a question. My view of a woman is not going to be the same as your view, so I don't want to prejudice your mind with any of my views."

"C'mon man."

"Sorry, but I can't sit here and describe a woman like that. Besides, it's demeaning."

"How?"

"Well, if I say something that isn't necessarily accurate, she can't defend herself."

"Jesus, it's always something with you. Okay, describe her in one word."

"Nubile."

"Nubile?"

"Yeah. Nubile."

"What the hell is that supposed to mean?"

"You don't know what nubile means?"

"Okay, I'll tell you what," I said. "Gimme an actress that she reminds you of."

"Uhh, Joan Severance."

"Who?"

"Joan Severance. She used to be a B-actress. You've never heard of her?" he asked, smiling.

Peppercorn was having fun with me, the way my cat did with bugs she caught around the house.

"Never mind," I said. "What does she do for a living?"

"Well, you'll get the wrong impression if I tell you."

"No I won't."

"I think you will."

"Look, you know that men don't really care what the woman does for a living, as long as she's got everything in working order and it's in the right place. As long as she's not, like, a hooker."

"She doesn't turn tricks," he said. "So it doesn't matter. Don't worry about it. Let her tell you."

"I'm just curious," I said. "I'm trying to get some sort of picture in my head of this girl, and a nubile Joan Severance just isn't doing it."

"Okay, but you promise you're not going to make a big deal of this?"

"Yeah."

"Okay. She's a castrator."

"What?"

"She makes horses into geldings."

"I don't believe this."

"That's where I met her—at the track. She's an assistant trainer. If you two hit it off, you have a line to a trainer. You know how cool that would be?"

I didn't.

* * *

Meanwhile, attacks on gas stations continued.

Gas station attacked; pumps destroyed by homemade bomb

Associated Press

DETROIT, MI—Four fuel pumps at an Exxon-Mobil gas station in Seed County were destroyed in an attack that occurred a little after midnight. The weapon appeared to be a makeshift yet sophisticated bomb, said Johnny Locomotive, county police chief.

"Based on the evidence collected at the scene, and the fact that the pumps blew up, we know that a bomb was used," Chief Locomotive said. "We're lucky the night-time worker turned off the pumps before he went home, or else it would have been raining gasoline for who knows how long."

Because of the use of the bomb, suspects face terrorism charges, Locomotive said. He added that since they targeted a national necessity in a time of war, they also face treason charges.

The owner of the station, Jack Grotsky, expressed remorse that he was not present when the attack took place.

"I wish I was there," Grotsky said. "I would have emptied my banana clip on those sons of [female dogs]."

Chapter Ten

Me and S.T.

Is there anybody you can trust these days? Yes there is.
—From "The Real S.T."

My job allowed me to meet a lot of new people. Old people, young people, white people, black people, scared people, aggressive people. I didn't think anything of most of these folks; I just wanted to do my job and go home. But one day, I came face to face with someone more important than I thought.

I'd heard about S.T. Youvie; I wouldn't forget a name like that, even if I wasn't sure what he did. Still, as far as I was concerned, he was another customer, one who had ordered a custom-made, state-of-the-art security system for the back door of the PIMBCO building, the very building in which I used to work. And as far as he was concerned, I was the menial, grey guy installing it.

As I walked inside, I noticed that the little outdoor patio where Jeff and I used to have lunch had been stripped of its table and chairs, and was barren. Even squirrels and birds avoided it.

A security guard directed me to a waiting area. There were pleather chairs around a round table that made the issues of *Time*, *Newsweek*, *Sports Illustrated*, and *Guns & Ammo* seem much more important than the one headline that was, incredibly, on each magazine—The Heat Is On! It referred to a heat wave in the southwestern U.S., a celebrity's espionage charge, the Miami basketball team, and a new kind of flamethrower.

Soon, a short man hurried over to me. He wore a pin-striped suit with American flag pins on each of his lapels, with American eagle cufflinks at his wrists.

"You're with the security people?" he asked.

"Yep."

"Okay," he said, not impressed. "This way."

He led me down a hall. Although we must have passed 10 people, nobody said anything or looked in our direction, as if they were told not to bother this guy.

"Are you a new business here?" I asked.

He stopped and looked at me. "Why are you asking?"

"Just curious," I said. "I used to know all the businesses in here."

"We're not in the business that, shall we say, needs a lot of advertising. We're a small, privately-owned operation, and would prefer if you simply not worry or think or mention anything to anybody. Okay?"

I have to say, I was a little intimidated by this little guy who seemed to want to make sure that I knew who was in charge here. He didn't have to try so hard, though, as I always let the customer know that he was in charge, and I was here to serve him. I did this because it made my job easier, not because I am any more subordinate than the next guy. My motives, much like the Decision Makers and the Lamkens and a whole lot of other people, were purely of self interest. But now, it was obvious this guy wanted me to know that he was the boss. Fine by me.

When we got to the back door, he stopped.

"Here it is," he said.

Here we are.

"This is what we want secured," he said, jerking his thumb toward a huge metal door.

"The back door?" I asked.

"That's right."

So I got to work, with this guy right over my shoulder. It didn't take long to install the system, and I was only interrupted once, by a barking voice that came through the guy's cell phone. The voice was so loud he held the phone away from his ear about two inches.

"S.T.! I'm going to need you to get over here pronto! I've got something else for you! Another job to take care of!"

"Okay, sir, sounds good."

"Listen S.T.! This can't wait."

"Okay, sir."

He sighed as he hung up. It was either one of relief or some kind of sexual supplication.

The state-of-the-art system had been equipped with sensors to detect motion and heat around the door and had microscopic video cameras at each corner. If anyone bothered it in any way, red spray paint and mace was released from tiny nozzles. The door could only be accessed with a code. If anyone punched in the wrong code, the door would automatically shut down and could only be opened with the key; which there was only one of; which couldn't be copied[21].

"S.T.!!!!" the barking voice shot through the phone. "Have you left yet?!"

"Uh, yes sir, I'm on my way," S.T. said, pushing his way past me. "I left five minutes ago."

* * *

Why did I go with Dubs Security for the door and not another company? Perhaps one run by Dylan Maderwood V or one of his colleagues? Simple. They offered us the best deal, and I was already over budget as it was.

—From "The Real S.T."

* * *

After work, I met Jeff and Celia at HaL's. When I came with Julie, there would always be at least twice as many people. I liked this smaller group better. Nothing was expected of me.

Celia sat at the bar watching muted television; Jeff threw darts.

"Hey Celia," I said.

"Grey!" she said, jumping up to give me a big hug. "How have you been? The house has been quiet without you."

"So what were you doing at PIMBCO today?" Jeff asked.

"Installing a custom-made security system on the back door," I said.

"Really? For who?"

"You're not going to believe this, but I think it was S.T. Youvie."

"The undersecretary for the Northeast Department of Energy Security?" Jeff asked.

"Yeah. He never introduced himself, and didn't have an ID badge, but I heard somebody on the phone yell that name a few times. If it was him, he didn't look like he does on television, but how many people have names like that, you know?"

As we talked, I noticed Celia wasn't paying much attention to us. She was making eyes with the bartender. If you squinted, he looked a tad like Colin Farrell. When she and Jeff finished their drinks, she went to get a couple more. She and the bartender laughed and leaned into each other, but then she abruptly grabbed her drinks and stormed back to us. She plopped down with a huff.

"You believe that fucking guy?" she said.

"What?" Jeff asked.

"He told me I looked familiar, so I said that I was almost on a survivor show, and told him about the movie they made about it, but he said he didn't watch much television. What an asshole."

"Maybe he was trying to pick you up," Jeff said, slightly amused.

"Well, he picked the wrong thing to say," she said.

Chapter Eleven

The Track

The way things are doesn't matter. The way things are doesn't know the difference between right or wrong. That's why the way things are are the way things are.
—Peppercorn

At the track, Pepper had a day gamblers wait their whole lives for. A *Let It Ride* day.

Well, the first part of the day, at least.

Here we are.

* * *

Pepper and I got to the track around noon. Just before we walked in, he turned to me. "I have a feeling something big is gonna happen today."

The first thing you notice at the track is desperation. It's palpable. People betting every second, screaming at little television monitors that lined the walls, reading numbers on the screens and in little books, cursing and ripping up tickets, slapping themselves on their thighs like jockeys, leaning back or forward to give their horses that added burst to hold off or nose ahead at the wire. When most people lost—and most people did—they looked completely and utterly shocked. You could tell that many had already counted their winnings before the race went off.

Here we are.

"So where is she?" I asked.

"Who?" he said, smiling.

"The nubile Joan Severance."

"Relax," Peppercorn said. "We just got here. Let's walk around, check out a couple races. Don't worry, you'll meet her."

Betting was done inside at a counter with tellers that reminded me of a bank. I guess that was appropriate, considering these people took your money. There were also two automated tellers like little ATM machines where you could place bets and cash tickets. These lines, which prevented human interaction with a live teller, were more crowded than the others.

After a few races, Peppercorn led me inside to the paddock. The smell of horse and fresh shit hit me, but wasn't at all disgusting. Stableboys walked these amazing creatures, 1,000-pound machines on toothpick legs, right around us. And I'd never really seen horses that close, dressed in silks and strutting around, look at me; but when they did, I swear they knew what was going on, and many of them seemed to enjoy it. Peppercorn said he loved looking at the horses, but I think he loved the horses looking at him even more.

As the Greek Mystique walked by me—and, I swear, did a little jig when the announcer called its name—I saw this red-haired young woman bending over in the corner. (Yes, I know what you're thinking—when I first laid eyes on Julie, she was also bent over. This was not the only way

I met women.) When she straightened up, she looked at me for a second, then saw Peppercorn and smiled.

Her hair was long and curly. She was a little taller than me, about 5'10" in work boots. Pale skin, which confused me, since I figured she spent a lot of time outdoors. Well, maybe not pale skin, like an unhealthy look—more like the color of a mannequin. Thin, though I could tell strength coursed through her lanky frame. Her mouth, nose, eyes were small, but her lips were full. Her bottom lip was chapped.

She had miraculously green eyes.

She walked over, petting horses, not at all concerned with me.

"Hey Pepper, how's it going?"

"Not too bad," he said. "How's the Mystique looking today?"

"Now, you know I can't answer that," she said with a smile. "If anybody overheard us, they'd think I was giving you inside information. And that wouldn't be good for me."

"I'm only teasing," he said. "I don't need any inside information. I brought my expert handicapper with me today," he said, nodding toward me. "He's so good, he doesn't even need a program."

"Is that right?" she asked.

"Vivian, I'd like you to meet Grey," Peppercorn said.

"Hi," I said.

"Good to meet you," she said. "So who do you like today?"

"What?" I asked.

"He likes the six in this race. And he likes a piece in the third at Belmont. Billy Mott on the grass."

"I'll have to remember that," she said, smiling.

Just then the alarm sounded for the race, but no horses were in the gate. People turned their heads this way and that, and the horses in the paddock jumped. Stableboys and trainers rushed to them, grabbing reins and stroking necks, diffusing the situation. It took a couple of minutes, and a hood had to be thrown over one the head of one horse who kept rearing up on his hind legs, to calm things down. It wasn't the most comfortable couple of minutes, though.

"What was that?" Peppercorn said. "Who the hell rang that bell?"

"It's the substitute track announcer," Vivian said. "That's the second time today he's done that. He's really spooking the horses."

"Where's the regular announcer?"

"Jim? He can't afford to drive to work anymore, so he started taking the bus, but then he complained that he was too clausterphobic to ride the bus, so he's on sick leave."

Here we are.

The movie *Let It Ride* is the story of Trotter, a lifetime gambler who would trade all of his losing yesterdays and tomorrows if he could only have a today when all the luck came his way. He gets a tip on a horse, wins a couple thousand on him, and continues to let all his winnings ride on horses for the rest of the day, winning each time. He can do no wrong; every bet he makes is golden.

Peppercorn hit his first bet, a win bet. "That's not always a good thing," he said. "Sometimes that's bad luck." But after he hit the second race, for another win bet and the Daily Double, he said, "It's time to take a shot."

He decided to play a Pick 6, the Holy Grail of horse racing.

It's a bet where you have to pick the winners of six straight races. Pepper rarely played it, saying, "It's hard enough to pick the winner in one!" That and the fact that the ticket alone can cost you. If you only pick one horse in each of the six races, the ticket will be two dollars. Hitting the bet with only one horse in each race is equivalent to hitting a Powerball lottery. You might as well play that.

To properly play a Pick 6, you need multiple horses in each race, which increases the cost of the ticket. Playing two horses in each race costs 128 dollars. After hitting the early races, Pepper figured he had enough money to take a shot.

He circled numbers in the Racing Form, talked to himself, squinted at the little television screens. The bet cost 256 dollars. He joked that he might be out after the first race.

He wasn't out after the first race.

Or the second.

When his closer came on at the very end of the stretch run of the third, putting him halfway home, he said, "We're halfway home." It was no longer, "*I'm* halfway home." He had thrown me in the mix with him.

"What do you mean me?" I asked. "I didn't give you any money."

"Doesn't matter. You must be my lucky star," he sang. "As long as you're here, you're on the clock."

The fourth race was a turf race, on the grass instead of dirt. Pepper was always the best on turf, and today was no exception. It wasn't even close. His horse led the entire way. Wire to wire. Only two more.

In the 20 minutes or so between races, I wasn't allowed to leave Pepper's side. It was funny that someone with so much gambling skill and knowledge would be superstitious. If I wanted to go to the bathroom, he stood at the urinal next to me. When I wanted something to eat, he waited in line with me.

We walked to the finish line before each race, during the post parade, to get a good vantage point. I asked Pepper why the "post parade," held before the race, wasn't called a "pre parade." He was distracted, and didn't answer.

The fifth race was tough, as both of Pepper's horses were ahead of the rest by a neck as they came down the stretch. The horse on the outside, Get Some, couldn't keep the pace and fell back. The horse on the inside, Hedontknowwhathesdoin, tried his best to stay in front. Suddenly, with only about 50 yards to go, a longshot from the back of the pack started running as if his ass was on fire and there was a pool in the winner's circle. He flew up the outside and passed every horse, even passed Hedontknowwhathesdoin. Pepper dropped to his knees. Neither of us said anything as we waited the five agonizing minutes for the photo finish to print, and when it did, Hedontknowwhathesdoin had won not by a nose, but a lip. Turns out the longshot didn't pass him until after the wire, and Pepper (and I) was one race away.

The last race was a thing of beauty. Pepper picked a horse, Schoolyard Bully, with a history of closing from way off the pace. In order for Schoolyard Bully to close like that, he needed the horses in front to set a quick pace. If they didn't, he didn't have a chance, as it would be unrealistic for a closer to make up ground on a front-running horse that didn't have to exert himself too much during the race and, therefore, would have plenty left in the tank.

But he also had a tactical horse in the race, Washyoubean, who liked to sit right off of the pace and make his move at the top of the stretch.

We didn't walk outside until the horses were in the gate. Neither of us said a word as Schoolyard Bully drifted all the way to the back, dead last, loping along while the other seven horses battled in front. Pepper couldn't see the quarter and half times, so we didn't know if the race was running fast or slow. When the horses hit the stretch, Washyoubean tried to rally, but had nothing. Two horses in front, the one and the three, pulled ahead, at least two horse-lengths in front of the field. I strained my head to spot Schoolyard Bully, and there he was, passing one horse...then another...then another.... With each stride he got closer and closer to the leaders. The only question was whether there was enough track left.

"Jesus Christ, these two are like Affirmed and Alydar!" Pepper yelled. "Run them down, Bully! Run them down!"

We ran alongside the horses as they thundered across the last 50 yards of track. Schoolyard Bully reached the two...came abreast with them both...and won by a head bob. It was close, but it was clear.

He'd hit it.

The Pick 6.

We were too amazed to speak. I didn't even know what how big a deal this was. I had no clue what he'd just won.

Then we looked at each other, and Pepper started laughing. Hysterically. He'd laugh for a minute, then go completely quiet, muttering something about "no objections please" and walking in little circles. I'd never seen him so...affected. He seemed, for the first time, a giddy bundle of nerves, nothing like the poised gambler I knew.

"Can you imagine what this is going to pay?" he asked as we made our way back to the paddock in a haze of emotion. "Oh my god, I can't believe it. I never even play these. What did I tell you? I told you that we were gonna have a good day! I told you! You're it! You're the key! You're coming with me from now on whenever I'm in a poker tournament, anytime I want to take a shot down the shore. I'm putting you on the payroll. Fuck security systems. We're gonna be famous! They're gonna make movies about us! You're the opposite of the cooler. You're the heater! Yes indeedie daddy-o, that's what the fuck I'm talking about!"

Fifteen minutes must have passed, because, though we didn't hear it, the call for the post parade rang out. As the horses walked the parade, an ear-shattering alarm sounded. Shrill. Shriller because people weren't expecting it.

The horses really weren't expecting it. The number-three horse, the favorite, took off for the paddock.

Horses are herd animals, and some argue that they are born with an instinct that refuses to allow them to be left behind the pack when running with others.

So what did the other horses do when they saw the number-three take off for the paddock? Coming at us were 11 charging horses, jockeys yanking on the reins in an attempt to control them.

The horses didn't stop. They'd had enough of the little men and women on their backs with their whips. They were running, and didn't care who or what was in their way.

I dove one way, Peppercorn dove another. He went the wrong way.

The first horse that hit him was the number-three horse, who went down to its front two legs before righting himself like Afleet Alex in the Preakness and running on. As I said, he was the favorite, and the public was dead-on. The other horses went right over him, one after another, not even breaking stride. By the time the closers crushed Peppercorn, he was dead.

Pepper once told me of a man who years ago bet his entire life savings that a horse named Dr. Fager, one of the greatest horses ever, would finish no worse than third in a race. He bet him to show. Dr. Fager won the race with ease, but it turned out that a jockey had filed an objection, and the track disqualified Dr. Fager, moving him down to fourth place. The old man clutched his chest, had a heart attack, and died on the track.

Now there was a new story, about the guy who died with a winning Pick 6 ticket in his hand. At least there would have been if people had known. As the crowd gathered around Pepper, I numbly plucked the ticket out of his hand and slid it into my pocket. I didn't even know how to cash the thing, but felt that I had to grab it.

After two weeks of desolation, desperation, and depression, I cashed the ticket. Partly for him, but 99 percent because I knew it was a lot of money. I didn't know how much, but when the teller told me I would have to come into the back office—for tax purposes and security—to collect my $76,837.30, I just nodded. There was no celebration or exclamation. Whatever.

I know that Pepper would've wanted me to cash the ticket. He wouldn't have hung around with someone so stupid as to not cash the thing.

Chapter Twelve
Death and a Misunderstanding

I never went to another cemetery for the rest of my life.
—Grey Reflections

I'd heard about the hole, the one in your stomach and heart and everywhere else, that arrives when a life close to you hops the trolley and ambles out of town. But a hole is empty, and what had taken residence inside of me was like a volcano spewing fire and loneliness and misery and ache for just one more conversation, one more afternoon, one more laugh.

What I got was a funeral.

"I'm very sorry for your loss," I said to Peppercorn's father after walking past the closed casket.

"You know, nobody believed me," he said. "I told everyone that it would be sunny today, partly cloudy at worst, but they kept saying it would rain. A storm was moving in, there were low pressure systems hovering over.... But it hasn't rained on the second Thursday in May after two days of showers in over 20 years.... I should have made them give me better odds, but I wasn't as focused as I'd normally be."

Peppercorn's father didn't say this to me, but to all who came up to him. And it didn't matter if someone walked away; he kept talking, the next person in line picking up the conversation baton from whomever was in front of him.

I didn't look at the casket. I never did. Inside was only a shell. The crab had crawled out and gone to its newest residence, wherever that was.

I remember what Peppercorn told me about death. We were drinking, and Peppercorn usually didn't talk about such matters. Said there was no point. But I asked him what he thought about death. He said: "We're these crumbs of cheese doodles spilled on the carpet. Some of us stay on the carpet longer than others. Some fall on the couch, and have a comfortable life. Some get eaten by the dog. Some get stepped on. Most get vacuumed up. And let me tell you—that vacuum bag needs a changing real bad."

This is what I think about death: No matter how fast you run, it always sits atop you, the best jockey in the world, whipping you down that stretch. And you get closer and closer to that finish line, but the closer you get, the more it moves back. And you want nothing more than to land in that winner's circle, and have your picture taken with roses slung around your neck, but you can't get to the finish line. And when you can't run anymore, you collapse, and have to be put down. Then you realize, maybe too late, that there is no finish line. And it's how you run the race.

And, if you're lucky, you get turned into glue, and hold something together. Or you become cheap dog food.

And you know how you'll end up after the dog eats you.

* * *

A bunch of people from the track showed, including Vivian. She wore a black blouse with reddish pants, boots and had a black band in her hair. She seemed so delicate, but then I remembered what she did for a living, and figured I should ask those horses how delicate she was.

If I make a joke while talking about Peppercorn's funeral, or if I was thinking of jokes while at Peppercorn's funeral, I don't want you to think that I'm trivializing his death in any way. He would have wanted me to think like that, to make jokes, as long as they were funny[22].

Vivian was alone. Jeff and Celia didn't stay, and Peppercorn was in the casket, so I was alone, too.

"Hi," I said.

"Hey."

"It's fucked up."

"Yep."

We watched mourners walk around the casket.

"Are you going to the cemetery?" she asked.

"No. Don't see a point."

"Me neither. I have to get back to work."

"Oh. Hence the boots."

"Yep. Well, I'll see you—"

"Hey listen," I said. "You think maybe we could, I don't know, get together some time? Maybe talk or something? Have a cup of coffee… I don't know, I'm not really good at this sort of a thing."

"Are you asking me out? At a funeral?"

"I don't know. It's just that…I don't know when the next time I'd see you again. And Peppercorn, you know, mentioned it to you, and to me, that we should, you know, get together, so I figured—"

"He never mentioned anything to me about you."

"What?"

"He never mentioned anything to me about you."

"Oh. Oh my god. I'm sorry. I thought he did."

"Nope."

"Oh. Wow. Well, this is bad then, I guess. I'm sorry."

"No, it's okay." She smiled at me. Not a big smile, but it was there.

I never went to another cemetery for the rest of my life.

By the front gate of the cemetery, a sign hung: "Recently purchased by Ptashkin, Solomon, and Brown," a company that fell under the entrepreneurial umbrella of Dylan Maderwood V, who knew how much money there was in death.

At a meeting on Lamken, Maderwood V said, "You know why there are fences around cemeteries? Because people are dying to get in."

Even though everybody had heard that joke many times before, they all laughed. They had no reason not to laugh. Life was good.

Chapter Thirteen

Plasma Death Ray

The Decision Makers all gardened—they all tended money. All of their thumbs were green.

—Grey Reflections

The Decision Makers gathered around a round table, on which were platters of food. A long buffet lined the west wall, arrayed with fresh fruits, cheeses, water, gourmet coffee, and coconut milk. Male and female Lamkens in loincloths, island dresses, blue jeans and t-shirts were on hand to wait on the Decision Makers. Classified Service agents watched, though not closely, the Lamkens. Outside the facility sat the only paved area of Lamken, a five-mile long stretch that served as the airport and road from the airport to the facility.

The Decision Makers had convened to discuss their secret weapon.

"Get S.T. on the phone," Maderwood V said.

In about 90 seconds, a large image of S.T. Youvie appeared on a theater-sized movie screen on the east wall.

"Good afternoon, S.T.," Maderwood V said.

"Good afternoon, gentlemen," S.T. said.

A few other Decision Makers snickered and whispered things like, "Gonnor-eeeee-ah," and "Siph-I-lusss," and "S.T.D." S.T. swore that he heard them, but what could he do?

"So, S.T.," Maderwood V said, "is everything secured?"

"Yes," S.T. said. "Things are all set. The code is safe in your personal computer."

"Good," Maderwood V said. "The Plasma Death Ray is locked and loaded. It can only be fired from this location with the access code."

"This is the most awesome weapon on the face of the planet," said Mathey III. "And the most efficient." Mathey III was very proud of Plasma Death Ray because, as it turned out, one of the companies of which he was a silent majority partner had engineered and manufactured it, just before it went bankrupt when it was discovered that no retirement money existed for anyone other than the Board of Directors or silent majority partners. Mathey's family had made a fortune selling weapons, all the way back to when they silently financed Samuel Colt.

"This thing is straight out of fucking Star Wars!" said Morsty IV. "It's controlled by a satellite—well, it pretty much is a fucking satellite—and shoots a plasma ray—like a giant laser—with extreme precision—as fine as a quarter in diameter, or as large as a mile—and fucking incinerates anything and everything in its goddamn path. I mean vaporizes it! They'll be nothing left. And there is no fallout. Or we can make as much fallout as we want. And there's no defense against it, because it can penetrate miles underground."

"Yes," said Mathey III. "What a work of science! How wonderful! You could, say, completely level and destroy the entire state of New York, while folks in Vermont wouldn't be affected at all."

"What if someone just destroys the satellite?" S.T. asked.

"That's the beauty," said Morsty IV. "Well, just one more mutherfucking beautiful thing about it—the satellite can withstand any attack—and I mean *any fucking attack*—except a plasma death ray!"

"So what happens if another country builds a Plasma Death Ray?" asked S.T.

"Well, for starters, nobody else knows about it. But even if they did, they couldn't launch it, because we've created this Plasma Death Ray to automatically detect any other Plasma Death Rays that are launched and instinctively destroy them before they can ever get fully operational."

"How were your scientists able to create such a thing?" Maderwood V asked.

"I'm not sure," Mathey III said. "They were paid a whole lot of money, so that may have had something to do with it."

"So it seems," said Maderwood V, "the country that controls the Plasma Death Ray has the world's military might."

"That is abso-fucking-lutely correct," said Morsty IV.

The other Decision Makers grabbed the cups that held the gourmet coffee and toasted their meeting. Although they all owned large shares of Beano Machino, they'd never actually drink it.

I was honored that Dylan entrusted me to install the launch code in his personal computer. It was safely tucked away behind the most technologically advanced computer security software known to man. There was no way to think that anyone could have breached that software. But that simply shows you that you can never be too careful.

—From "The Real S.T."

Chapter Fourteen

Closer

She smiled sweetly at me, and I felt all funny inside.
—Grey Reflections

During this time, Vivian and I got closer. It was glorious drawing together—the sleepless nights of wondering if she really liked me, of not being able to eat, of suffering from nervous bowel syndrome when I was trying to install security systems (I mean, you can only tell customers so many times that you have to make sure the flush of the toilet won't disrupt the system before the homeowners look at you funny). I tell you, there's nothing like falling in love.

Our first date lasted 17 hours. I picked her up at seven; we left the restaurant at 10; got back to my place at 11; got in bed around five in the morning; slept from six-thirty to eight-thirty; got back to her place around nine; had coffee; looked at photos; I left at noon.

We didn't have sex; in fact, not one article of clothing came off. Except for our socks. And I'm embarrassed to say that my feet were not pedicured, and I gouged her a few times with my box-cutter big toenail. When she didn't leave after that, I knew it was something special.

I was now driving, too. I got Peppercorn's car. His parents gave it to me. They said I should have it, and they didn't want to go through the hassle of selling.

Even dead the guy hooked me up.

Vivian and I had dinner, and kissed, and fumblingly ran our hands over each other's bodies, and saw movies, both artsy ones at the Ritz (before that was shut down) and action ones at the multiplex, and went to Dairy Queen, and had laughs and teased each other. She began working more on farms in Chester County and with trainers and breeders from Delaware Park, to be closer to me.

Our first sex session wasn't the most romantic, performed by two participants who didn't seem to have had much practice recently (at least with a live, new partner). I finished before I'd even got in[23]; Vivian just touched my soldier at arms when it spouted like a fountain. Maybe it was because my dick was so fearful of the castrator's touch that her hand was uncontrollably sexy. So we had to wait almost 10 minutes, which got progressively more uncomfortable as each second passed, until I was ready to set sail once again.This time my ship found land ripe and juicy, which got juicier the further I explored, until finally, where the atmosphere was at its most moist, the rainforest of love, if you will, I plunged into something so wonderful it convinced me it was the Fountain of Youth.

As we were doing our thing, Vivian suggested some music. All I had was my bedside alarm clock[24]. Turning it on gave us, fortuitously, some Marvin Gaye.

Then the station went to a commercial break.

I'm sure you know how sex goes. I guess mine wasn't any more graphic that what you have, or at least (I hope) what you fantasize about. But it was mmm, mmm, good.

The more we did it, the better we got. And we did a lot of it. Soon, we were old pros.

"You can tell a lot about somebody by what's in their medicine cabinet," Vivian said one morning she slept over. We were getting ready to go to breakfast. I love breakfast—always have. I'd much rather go out on a breakfast date than dinner.

"You go through people's medicine cabinets?" I asked.

"Sure. You don't?"

"Oh, absolutely. I'm just surprised you do."

"I think you can learn even more by what reading material is in the bathroom."

As Vivian got ready, I laid on my back, looking at the ceiling, arms behind my head. I made the mistake of contemplating how great life was right now. I was making money hand over fist installing these simple yet effective security systems, the workings of which I didn't even understand; I was having crazy monkey sex with this redheaded firecracker who smoldered innocence, if such a thing is possible; and...well, that was about it, but that's really all a guy needs to have a wonderful wonderful life. What the hell did I care about some energy bullshit? Why should I care that gasoline was expensive? Money come, money go, as Peppercorn said. Besides, gas and oil and energy were part of the larger world, the real world, the one that didn't care about me, or ask for my opinion, or make a decision based on how it might affect me. See, I didn't live in the real world. I lived in a duplex apartment in Media.

"So what does it say about someone who has Maxim and the Big Book of One-Liners in his bathroom?" Vivian asked.

"Um, probably that the person likes to look at airbrushed women in various states of undress," I said, "and, uh, that he likes to pull out these one-liners at parties and work and make people think that he just made them up."

Turns out Vivian wasn't solely looking for things to find out about me. She was checking to see if I had any painkillers. Percocet, specifically. At this point, I didn't know that she was addicted to those things. She had a prescription for them, due to a back injury suffered years before when she was thrown from a horse. Since she could only get the script filled once a month, she often ran out before she could renew the bottle.

So she looked for them.

* * *

"When you smile, things inside of me go off," I said the next morning at breakfast.

She smiled, we held hands, and things inside of me went off.

* * *

We were on the couch watching something on tv[25]. The couch was a three-seater with a recliner on one end, old, kinda rough, that I got from a customer. Vivian had just drifted off to sleep. My head, which she'd been rubbing, lay in her lap. She wasn't nearly as good at Julie as rubbing my head, but what are you going to do? She made up for it in other ways, like civility and faithfulness.

My eyes got heavy, and as I straddled sleep and awareness, our breathing patterns synchronized. Same inhale, same exhale, same amount of air, same pause between repeating.

How about that?

* * *

While Vivian and I grew close, things weren't going so great between Jeff and Celia. Apparently, she was disappointed in him for not being what she wanted, and even more disappointed in herself for not being what she wanted. So she'd unload all of her frustrations and abuse at Jeff.

How did I learn this? I read it in Celia's tell-all blog, once she became semi-regionally-famous.

Celia came in mid-conversation with her coworker, Heather, remarking at how she'd eventually get on a reality show. She knew she'd be perfect; she only needed a break.

"You would be perfect, Celia," Heather said. "You really would."

For Heather, agreeing with Celia was nothing out of the ordinary. She agreed with anyone who talked to her, never wanting to make waves or disappoint. As a young girl, she accidentally killed the family dog by feeding it a large chocolate Easter bunny. She thought it was good thing, especially when she saw how the dog gobbled up that bunny. The dog didn't know any better, either; he simply ate until he couldn't eat anymore. Literally. Heather's mother never forgave the little girl for her mistake: Heather became the reason why her mother got fired from her job at the deli, even though she was stealing lunch meat; her mother also blamed Heather for her older sister's cocaine habit.

How did I know this about Heather? During the short stint I lived at Jeff and Celia's, Celia came home from work almost every day talking about her. I listened. I don't think Jeff did.

"Relationships are hard."

That's what Celia's blog said.

"You want them to work, but sometimes things just don't work out the way you want them to. So many people who fall in love with others change, and then you wake up and look at the person sleeping next to you and say, 'Who is this person? This isn't who I fell in love with. What the hell are you doing here, and where is the other guy?' When this happens, you have every right to be angry, and to take out that anger on this new person now in your bed.

"Besides, people change. I've grown enough to realize that. We're just not the same people we were yesterday, and there's a good chance we're not going to be the same people tomorrow that we are today. Until we realize that, I don't think we will ever truly be happy."

Quite philosophical.

Jeff wasn't enough for her. He didn't provide enough attention, enough excitement, enough.

To Jeff, life was boring. But that wasn't bad. That was life. Routine. With a side of routine. With a little routine for dessert. He used to joke and say exciting lives weren't better, because you never knew what would happen day to day. "If you want excitement, find a different way to eat every day. Try living without a stable income. You'll have plenty of excitement."

She'd get mad and say he didn't know what he was talking about.

Chapter Fifteen
How I Met Thanloc's Mother

In the business world, you never know who you're going to meet, so you better make sure you fake it each minute of every day.
—Grey Reflections

The day I met Thanloc and his mother turned out to be the most important day of my life up to this point[26], and will most likely be the most important day of my life after this point[27].

The Gladwyne stop was my second of the day. I'd just come from installing a basic security package at a brick home in Havertown, a suburb about seven minutes from West Philadelphia. The homeowners had decided they wanted to upgrade from an aluminum bat and golf club to a security system and Glock. They asked me if I could help them with the gun. They seemed disappointed when I said I couldn't, and never gave me the coffee they promised.

The house where Thanloc and his mother lived was unassuming and small compared to some of the other monstrous, showy Main Line homes. This house seemed like it wanted nothing more than to be ignored, with basic, waist-high bushes ringing the rose-less yard.

It was a single, with vanilla ice cream color siding and bland brown shutters and doors.

Before I knocked, the door opened. A woman whose age I never could have guessed answered the door. She had the most gorgeous skin I had ever seen. Behind her was, I guessed, her son. He had the same skin. Their eyes were calm, yet expressed a loneliness. The son's, especially, carried a secret, and when he saw me, sparked like a lighter low on butane.

"Good morning. Sorry I'm late. Traffic is a mess."

"Welcome," the mother said. "You are not late. We knew you'd come."

"Well, Dubs'll never let you down."

"Come in. I am Kala, though you can call me Karla, if you'd like. This is my son, Thanloc."

"Good to meet you both," I said. I handed them my card. They both smiled before looking at it, and when they read they card, they became almost giddy.

I was there for three hours, about two-and-a-half longer than the job should have taken. They asked more questions than any customer had ever asked, about things I had no idea about (because I was installing the systems, I should have known all about them. But questions didn't come up as often as you might think, because people mainly didn't care how things worked, and worried more about if they worked.).

"Will the security system protect against intruders?"

"Only if it's on," I answered.

"Will it keep out unwanted people, no matter how hard they'd like to get in?"

"As long as the doors and windows are shut and locked, and the system is on."

"Could you secure a larger house?"

"Absolutely," I said. "The bigger the better."

"What about something massive," Thanloc asked, "like a city?"

"No problem," I answered, figuring if there were anything like that to secure, Dubs would find a way to make it happen, considering how much we'd be able to charge. "So you can throw your worries out the window," I said, giving them the same lines I gave all of my customers. "In fact, just wait until you see how carefree your lives are knowing that you are nestled as safely as the president of the United States. It'll be like you're on your own little island, far away from everyone else."

When I finished, the mother muttered something in another language. Thanloc hugged me and said, "You are the one we were waiting for."

"Well, you're very welcome," I said, not used to this much of a thank you. "Just doing my job." I pulled out the invoice. "Here's the total cost. You can send all payments to the address at the bottom. If I can just get your signature here, and here, and initial here and here, I'll be on my way."

"We will see you soon, Grey," Thanloc said.

I thought they were happy because I made them safe. I didn't know how important I was to their story.

Even though Los' vision said a "gray" man, and I was "Grey," it was close enough.

Thanloc was more confident than his Lamken cousins in America. They were similar to other late-teen early 20s Americans in that they hung out, and spoke to each other on the phone and on Web cams, and emailed, instant messaged, and texted each other. They didn't say too much or gossiped—the Lamkens are not and never were an overly talkative people. I think that's a shame, considering how many languages they speak.

I didn't know then, but I know now, that the Lamkens—all around 20, three boys and one girl—were well read. Everything they got their hands on. They were tremendously athletic, especially at running, and would have shattered cross country and distance races for local high schools and colleges without batting an eye. The reason why they didn't participate in organized sports? The Elders repeatedly told them never to showcase their full talents. They didn't want them drawing attention. See, aside from their incredible skill at mastering languages, Lamkens also have the incredible ability not to be noticed. A lot of people in America hate that, and will do almost anything to stand out of the crowd. The Lamkens did all they could never to soar above any radar.

And although I didn't know it at the time, Thanloc was the greatest computer hacker I had ever met. Okay, he was the only computer hacker I'd ever met. When you think about Lamkens and their linguistic prowess, it was no surprise at how easily Thanloc mastered computer languages. All he needed to hack were the proper resources—there was nothing he couldn't do with computers.

Here we are.

Part IV

Chapter Sixteen

Rallies

The rallies, of course, couldn't remain peaceful. It's not the American way.

—Grey Reflections

Historically, Americans expressed their displeasure at ruling factions of society by banding together, resulting in a wave of energy that crashed down upon the repressors.

One of the most common forms of this culminating energy was a rally, which had been much more popular before 1980. After that, distractions distractions distractions, and people didn't feel the need to bother with rallying.

Until now.

The once-dead practice experienced a resurrection. People communicated on the Internet across counties, cities, states, setting up rally points for anything and everything.

Some rallies, like the one to stop naming children after nouns, drew only a handful of people.

Others, like those for affordable health care, or to move troops from one country to another, drew more.

Many times there would be incentives to attend rallies, like food and drink and music.

There even was a rally against the color-coded Terror Alert System, which was unveiled after 9/11 with much fanfare, but forgotten after a year or so. I only remember the Code Red Rally because Mountain Dew representatives were on hand handing out free 20-ounce bottles of their Code Red drink, which made the rallyers crazy for awhile. After the caffeine and sugar rush ended, though, rallyers crashed, shuffled away harmlessly, held their heads and sucked on candy to get the bitter taste out of their mouths.

Up until this point, I'd never been to a rally. I don't think any of them missed me.

Likewise, none of the Decision Makers had ever gone to a rally.

I don't think they were missed, either.

* * *

One rally did draw major attention—because of the outcome rather than the cause. It took place in Camden, New Jersey, a tremendously volatile city whose number one exports were heroin and rigor mortis.

The drug motivated three groups to gather. The first group, after hearing that the heroin so many flocked to Camden to get was cut with the blood thinner fentyanol, causing lots of deaths to lots of users, marched and shouted. They weren't too organized, and didn't shout the same words, but the basic effect was, "Oh shit! I got to get me some of that!"

They were hungry, scrawny, pissed off, and looking for a fix, but they were, incredibly, peaceful. That is, until they ran into a group of heroin dealers rallying against the practice of cutting heroin with fentyanol. The dealers were clever enough to realize that if their customers dropped dead, they more than likely wouldn't purchase any more.

Then came the third set of rallyers, the fentyanol pushers. They marched under the strict teachings of capitalism, arguing that all they did was provide consumers with what they wanted. Why should they be punished if their product caused the ground to consume a few consumers? That wasn't their fault, and it certainly wasn't hurting business. They had a right to march for their cause. After all, this was America, not communist China or dictatorial Venezuela or one of those really crazy countries in the Middle East.

The three groups stared at each other, not knowing what to do. They may have dispersed quietly and quickly, but never got the chance. The driver of a news helicopter, who should have been reporting the traffic situation on the Ben Franklin Bridge but had taken a wrong turn above I-76 and wound up above Camden, saw the milling masses below and radioed back to the station, who quickly dispatched a camera crew to the scene. Other stations heard this over their police scanners and sent crews of their own. The police, hearing the report a few minutes later, sent four cruisers; but by the time they arrived, it was too late.

The straight heroin dealers made a beeline for the users, who made a mad dash toward the fentyanol pushers, who rushed to the straight heroin dealers. When all three mixed, mayhem ensued.

People were shoved to the ground, trampled on, grabbed at whatever they could, ran away, threw weak punches. It didn't take long until leaders of the fentyanol and straight heroin gangs met face to face in the middle of the pack.

That's when the guns came out.

That's when the news people almost creamed in their pants.

When the smoke and smack cleared, six people had been shot, and 13 people had shot up.

The rally—or, rather, the outcome—led the local news that evening, and even made national headlines.

People pretty much forgot about it by the next commercial break.

* * *

Then rallies for lower gas prices popped up. You may even say that a movement began. If so many people didn't have to drive to attend them—many from more than 30 miles away—they could have attracted even larger crowds.

* * *

The Decision Makers watched the rallies on FOX News at their homes, on Lamken, or at exclusive country clubs. They found it great entertainment, the epitome of American expressionism.

S.T., though, saw that the rallies could potentially be a problem. He said as much during a conference call.

"S.T., stop worrying so much," Maderwood V said to the image of S.T. on the enormous screen. "This is good old fashioned American discourse and dialogue. This is what separates us from other countries, who burn effigies and throw rocks and blow things up. Our people do it peacefully—they let their voices be heard, and then they go back to work. We should encourage these things, to show how civil our society can be even when people disagree."

"Yes, I understand that, but studies say that if the demonstrators' causes are not heard, or if they don't see the change they wish to see, they will move onto the next phase, which is action."

"You see what I mean?" Maderwood V asked the other members of his round table. "He's just a boy. He hasn't been in this business long enough to understand how things really work." Maderwood V tended to do this when he wanted to embarrass someone. He'd talk like a father asking his wife what to do with their child.

"Well, I warned you this might happen when you gave him this job," said Menginth IX, struggling to open a pistachio. "All of the qualities that one needs to succeed cannot be learned; some you must be born with. I wonder if your boy comes equipped with all of the intangibles."

"Maybe you're right," Maderwood V said. "Maybe I was wrong in taking a chance on him."

"No no no no no no," said S.T. "It's not that." As he spoke, he felt a terrible stabbing in his side, causing him to double over.

"Bowing is a good start," said Mathey III. "Maybe he isn't that bad after all. I think there's hope for this lad."

S.T. righted himself, trying to ignore the pain, which only came when he breathed. "Thank you sirs," he gasped.

S.T. disappeared from the screen, the Decision Makers fading from his view. He walked to the small bathroom in the basement of the PIMBCO building, popped a couple of acid reflux pills, and looked in the mirror.

His problem wasn't acid reflux, but a large ulcer that caused his stomach to bleed. In fact, he'd been doubling over for a couple of weeks now, at home and at work. Rose offered no sympathy. In fact, she didn't even think he was in pain. She thought that he was bending over to tie his shoes.

Though he wanted more than anything else to become a Decision Maker, S.T. didn't know there was no way he'd ever sit in that room. As Pepper may have said, he had a better shot at getting pregnant. None of the Decision Makers respected him; he didn't have a Jr. or III or IV or V after his name; he had not nearly enough greenbacks; and he didn't have the right initials[28].

Speaking of getting pregnant, all Rose was a baby. But no matter how hard she and S.T. tried, a pregnancy didn't happen.

Rose and S.T. pretty much only tried in the beginning of their marriage. The whole sex thing was still novel enough to make S.T. crave his woman every night, the smell from her vagina never bothering him in the least.

Once the novelty wore off, though, sex became work to S.T. And since he wasn't receiving money or power, the work ceased being worth it. So he concentrated his energies into work that resulted in money and power.

Rose, though, needed more than just an occasional prick. She was a woman in the prime of her life; and besides, S.T. was the only man she had ever met who wasn't turned off by her uniqueness, which fueled her passion even more.

She opened herself sexually to S.T. like she had to nobody before, but he didn't know what to do with it. So she strayed, reverting to her teenage years of sleeping with pretty much whoever could stand her funkiness. Guilt never affected her, since she felt her un-fragrance owed her.

S.T. had no idea. He's not even sure he would have cared even if he did know. He was too busy obeying orders and becoming a very important person in America. He was learning from the best in the business, and couldn't be bothered with marital responsibilities.

But all of Rose's affairs withered shortly after they began. None of her cuck-a-dees could stay after getting too many whiffs of her flower.

* * *

I mentioned that Celia had fallen into a rut. So she did something to spice up her life that she never thought she'd do.

She went to a rally.

She didn't hide the reason why she went—she did it because she read in *People Magazine* that rallies were the new cause célèbre for celebrities. She didn't even remember what the cause was. She remembers being far too overdressed, but that people stared, pointed, and nodded in her direction. She got a thrill.

Her designer sunglasses cost more than what most of the rallyers made in a week. Her heeled shoes made it difficult to navigate through the swarm of bodies that, truth be told, didn't smell all that great.

But as she was looking for the refreshment tent, she was hit with a realization of why she was there.

She saw the news van, and Channel 6's own Jane Creamer, live on the scene. Jane was reviewing with her cameraman the shots that she wanted and discussing with an assistant producer what to say. Celia watched as the group set up, and then Jane took the mic, did a quick hair and makeup check, and started reporting.

"We're live here on Vine Street, where hundreds—maybe even thousands—have lined the streets for a peaceful yet powerful protest. The hardworking citizens of this great city will not let their voices be denied, and want the folks in Harrisburg and Washington to know that if their rally falls on deaf ears, then come voting season, the rallies of the politicians will also go unheeded."

Celia knew that, if given the chance, she could do a better job than Creamer. Why hadn't she thought of the news before?

* * *

New York Post

Shootout at gas station kills three, wastes fuel, prompts National Guard

Brooklyn—A shootout at a gas station in Brooklyn between would-be robbers and a clerk left one robber, the clerk, and a customer dead. One of the bullets punctured a gas pump, spilling more than 100 gallons of gasoline.

The shootout has prompted the undersecretary of Energy Security, S.T. Youvie, to deploy the National Guard at various gas stations in the Northeastern United States. Speculators claim that the deployment will cause oil prices to skyrocket, though their reasons backing that claim are, at best, speculations.

Also, the owner of the station claimed that the spilled gasoline will cause prices to rise.

I refused to let the American people be their own enemy. They needed to be policed. At least in my quadrant.

—"The Real S.T."

Chapter Seventeen

Dream Jockey

I'll either come back a bum or a king—and I'm feeling regal today, boy.
—Peppercorn, while living

When he first came to me in a dream, I thought I was dreaming. I mean, dreaming in the dream. He started out far away, nothing more than a speck that got slightly bigger as it neared. When the speck matured to a form, I saw that it was bouncing up and down. When the bouncing got closer, I saw that it was someone riding a horse. Even before the form reached me, I knew it was Pepper.

"How goes it, my good man?" he said.

"What the hell are you wearing?" I asked. He was dressed like a jockey, in red and white silks, with red polka-dots on his white shorts.

"You like? I picked it out myself."

His horse, a beautiful reddish steed, snorted and shook its head.

"Yeah, Secretariat doesn't like it. He wanted me dressed in his Derby colors—blue and white. But when I saw how this outfit complemented my complexion, I just had to have it."

"Wow. So this is Secretariat, huh?"

"Yeah. Isn't he great? I get to ride anybody I want. So far I've been on Cigar and Smarty Jones, and I'm getting on Dr. Fager next. But Ruffian is my favorite. She has so much in her, Grey, she could have been as good as any of them."

"That's just dynamite," I said.

I looked around and, for the first time, noticed I was on a dirt racetrack. The grandstand was to my right, and the infield was just to my left. In fact, I was leaning against the rail.

"So I guess things are going pretty well for you right now," Pepper said, still on the Secretariat.

"Can't complain."

"Things heating up with Vivian, I see."

"Yeah, she's great. We're having—what do you mean, you see?"

"I can see a lot of things. For instance, when you guys are getting down to sex, what you should do is—"

"Yo!" I said. "What the fuck are you doing watching me have sex?"

Pepper laughed. "I'm not, man, I'm just fucking with you. Man, it's still great messing with you."

We were no longer the only ones here. The grandstand was slowly but steadily filling with fans.

"Ok, we gotta wrap this up," he said.

"Wrap this up? What the hell are you talking about? What's going on here?"

"What do you mean what's going on here? What does it look like? It's a race."

"A race? What the fu—isn't this *my* dream?"

"If it is, you better tell me what the trifecta's gonna be, so I can make some money."

Just then two horses loped by.

"Man O'War looks strong, but he hadn't seen Big Red yet. Oh shit, is that Damascus? We'll have to watch out for him too."

"All right man," I said. "It was really good seeing you."

"I'm not done yet. I got something to tell you."

"Yeah I know, make sure I bet smart and strong."

"Not that, asshole. Though I must admit it's good to see that you've learned a little since I've been gone. What I want to tell you is to watch out. Be ready for things that are going to happen, especially in the next couple of months. And believe in the vision."

"What vision? What am I going to see?"

"It's not *your* vision," he said. "It's the vision that you will hear—that's what you have to believe."

"Vision that I will hear? What the hell does that mean?"

"I can't tell you much more," he said as the horn went ber-ber-BER-BER-BER-ber-ber-ber-ber-ber-berrrrr, ber-ber-ber-BER-BER-BER-BER-ber-ber-ber-ber-berrrrrrrr. "Besides, I gotta get in the post parade."

"But you can't just tell me to trust the vision. I need more than that."

"I'd love to tell you more, but I can't. Truth is, I don't even know. I can only see a few pages ahead. Believe me, it'll be the best thing that ever happened to you—even better than cashing that Pick 6 ticket."

"Guess you know about that, huh?"

"Of course I do. And if you didn't cash it, I would've haunted your ass for the rest of your life for being so fucking stupid."

"Can you really haunt people?" I asked.

"I don't know. I haven't signed up for any of the classes yet."

With that, Pepper pulled on the reins and Secretariat trotted to the post parade. As he got smaller, he called out over his shoulder.

"Oh, one last thing. Bet the four horse in the fifth at Churchill tomorrow. It's a lock."

The weirdest thing was that I didn't wake up right after the dream, yet still remembered everything in vivid detail. It was good to see Pepper again, if only for a short time.

I didn't understand his message. But I kept his words somewhere between the back and front of my mind, resting their eyes.

The next day I went to the track to see Vivian. I bet $100 to win on the four horse in the fifth race at Churchill. It went off at 9-1 and got out of the gate great.

It finished dead last. I swore I heard Pepper laughing as I ripped up the ticket.

Chapter Eighteen

The Water Mark

The water mark, if it rises high enough, will drown a lot of people.
—"The Real S.T."

"I'd like to call this meeting to order," said Mathey III.

The Decision Makers laughed, as they always did when one of them made a joke, even if it wasn't funny[29]. Mathey III always started their meetings with this announcement.

"I'd like to turn things over to our great friend, partner, and businessman, a man you all know and love, Mr. Dylan Maderwood V."

Everyone clapped little golf-claps. They were happy. No matter what went on in the world, everything was peachy-keen.

"A product in high demand," said Maderwood V, "tightens supply, raises prices. Capitalism is my favorite science. And science builds on itself. Of course, our country should lead the charge in alternative sources of energy. After all, those sources, once bottled, will be high in demand."

"How long will it take for those sources to be bottled?" asked Morsty IV.

"Oh, we have things ready. I propose we unveil them in 10 years. That would give plenty of time to work out any kinks."

If the Decision Makers or their Classified Service agents had been paying closer attention, they would have seen Lamkens listening intently to everything being said—had been listening intently for quite some time. Well, I guess it's not entirely fair to say that the Decision Makers had let their guard down. Fact was, the Lamkens had gotten so good at camouflaging their actions that nobody could have determined what they were doing. Lamkens scribbled facts, spoke to each other in different languages—even bird calls. The Decision Makers and guards thought they were taking food orders or discussing the best way to clean up. Which was, after all, their job, and for which they were paid an extreme amount of money—hell, they were given a money-printing machine.

"Get S.T. on the screen," said Maderwood V.

In seconds, S.T.'s prostrated body appeared. He forced himself upright. His mouth was ringed with dried pink, remains of Pink Bismuth, two bottles of which he chugged per day.

"So, S.T.," said Morsty III, "did you gobble up your mutherfucking lunch?"

"Uh, excuse me?" S.T. seemed surprised.

"You have shit on your mouth."

The Decision Makers laughed as S.T. wiped away the dried Bismuth. Their laughter caused him more stress, and he doubled over again.

"That's okay, S.T.," said Maderwood V. "You don't have to bow."

"Actually, I was—"

"We've Decided that you will institute a 10-year plan," said

Maderwood V, "outlining how the country can best address this energy situation the newspapers and televisions are talking so much about."

The Decision Makers were masters of the 10-year, and nine-year, and eight-year plan.

"The public needs to know that in order to make energy reliable and safe for the environment, it needs to be purified and refined, which isn't cheap. More money has to be spent on making sure energy is clean and efficient, which means that prices must fluctuate."

S.T. nodded and jotted notes. He'd be responsible for carrying out Maderwood V's vision. That's usually how Maderwood V—well, I'll let S.T. tell it.

* * *

"I've heard critics say that I was nothing more than a yes-man, Dylan Maderwood V's puppet. But people don't realize how much I did. I was the conduit between Dylan's brainstorms and their results. I was responsible for transforming his ideas into reality, thoughts into action.

Why me? Because I had the most important quadrant of the country. People still may think the South runs the country, as they elect the president—but even the president gets a paycheck, which somebody has to sign[30]*.*

*Critics also say that these Decision Makers were nothing more than a bunch of dodder-headed rich kooks. That couldn't be further from the truth. For instance, Dylan was an extremely well-read man, especially in philosophy. He liked to consider himself a Plato for the 21*st *Century, and that his ideas were ideals. He was outside of the cave, and it was his duty to lead as many people out as he could. Failing that, he would illuminate the walls of the cave so that people inside could watch something and be* *happy, not worry about existential things like existence and equality and justice and happiness. It was my job to create realities, to put plans into motion.*

After all, you can only force people to think a certain way by being very very persuasive.

—From "The Real S.T."

"People need to know that the problem is being addressed," said Maderwood V. "They also need to understand that a solution cannot be rushed, if they want the solution to be right. Throw in some distractions, and people'll forget about it after a while."

* * *

Meanwhile, the American people drafted their own plans. They communicated mostly online, through social networking sites like, Facebook, MySpace[31], Twitter and Youtube videos. They planned "No Gas Days" and rallies for cheaper gas. Sites were marked and calendar dates were circled; but when it came down to it, the number of people who said they'd participate was greater than the amount of people who actually walked the walk.

The first "No Gas Day" was so poorly received that it never even counted. So the second "No Gas Day" was labeled as the first "No Gas Day." This time, even more word got out. Internet, graffiti, bulk text messages and emailing. Articles in free city papers were read by 16 people, making them the most-read items in city paper history.

Thousands of people under 25 years of age had to call out of work that day—they refused to take public transportation and couldn't stand their coworkers nearly enough to car pool. Basic food, contracting, landscaping, and other menial services grinded to a halt. But adults had to go to work. They couldn't be bothered with a cause.

So the "No Gas Days" didn't really do anything except make the young folk feel as if they were doing something.

* * *

The gas crisis affected everything. Food cost more, because it cost more to ship. Prices were so high that condiment sandwiches began appearing on menus. Relish on a roll was popular. As was water ice and pretzels. Sometimes people had it without the ice and pretzels.

Some really poor people starting eating dirt. With salt and pepper, if they were lucky.

One day, as Mengith IX was being chauffeured home, construction forced his Town Car to detour through a neighborhood where a group of people protested at a gas station.

"How could anyone have a problem with this country, especially if they live in it?" he asked, chuckling at the incredulity of his rhetorical question.

* * *

"This shit is really starting to get to me," Vivian said.

"Well, you should watch where you're standing," I replied, nodding toward the horse manure that surrounded us.

"I mean, what are we supposed to do? All I'm trying to do is what I want, what I like. I'm not looking to make millions. I like what I do, and accept less money because of it. But it's getting hard for me to live. I can't even afford to drive anymore."

She deftly saddled and looped reins around a horse who was recovering from the dreaded operation that will ensure he never gets put out to stud. Since he'd been acting up before races, and was so hard to control, he needed to be made into a gelding. Chop chop, stop cock.

"What can we do?" I asked. "Everybody complains about the weather, but nobody does anything about it."

"People will get together. Something's gotta give. I can hardly get down to Delaware Park anymore. And forget about Colonial. The trailers can't go back and forth as much as they used to. I'm working longer hours, losing money. It isn't right."

"It's a shame people don't have the power anymore," I said, trying to ease some of her worry while overlooking her concern.

"I know," she said. "That is a shame."

I put my arms around her, kissed her. She kissed back. It was nice how we could ignore everything with a simple—

"I mean, it just drives me fucking crazy," she said, stepping out of my arms. "If everyone came together, we could change it. The government or whoever's in charge would have to change. They'd have no choice."

"I know," I said. "But that's the problem. Getting everyone to unite on anything is next to impossible. People have too much going on." Like me, who was standing in a field of horse shit while my girlfriend worked.

"What about the rallies?" she asked. "What about the "No Gas" days? More people are joining each one. Don't tell me you don't think they'll change anything."

Her optimism was so sexy.

"I don't know. I haven't really thought about it, I guess. And maybe we won't know the impact they had until time passes. And most people can't wait that long."

I didn't realize it then, because I needed time to pass, but that was one of the most profound things I ever said.

"Would you help me scrape the shit off of Lil Theatrical's shoes?" Vivian asked, nodding toward a horse which I heard cost over one million dollars. That's some pretty expensive shit.

Then she popped two Percocets.

I loved Vivian's physical and emotional flaws. I don't know why. I found myself attracted to Julie's flaws as well. Perverse, but true.

When she was on the percs, she was wonderful to be around. When not, she could be nasty. Real nasty.

Though thin, she had a bit of cellulite on her ass and thighs. And a little vein that ran from the inside of her right nostril to her lip—it was barely visible, and not at all unless you got really close. But she was self-conscious about it. I found that out the hard way one night in bed.

"I like that little vein."

"I hate it."

"Why? I think it's cute."

"I hate it, okay? Don't talk about it." At which point the bed froze up like an old penguin's pussy.

Maybe I loved their flaws because I knew how fucked up I was. Or something like that.

The fact that she popped pills isn't why I'm now stating how attracted I was to her flaws. It just seems to fit at this point, and I didn't want to force it anywhere else.

And even though I found myself attracted to her flaws, I think at this point, our relationship was beginning to fray. I know, I know, it doesn't seem like a story-book romance—we didn't even make it through a year. I guess it was a flash fiction romance.

Aren't people reading less nowadays, anyway?

Chapter Nineteen

Land Is Not Free—Gotta Pay the Rent

After all, Americans were not meant to use public transportation.
—Grey Reflections

Saturday, in Jeff's office. It was sweltering, the air conditioner off, the company cutting back on utility bills. Outside, Market Street filled with an unorganized energy rally. Signs read, "I shouldn't have to eat Taco Bell for cheap gas!" and "Home of the Free, Gas of the Rich" and, my favorite, "Honk for lower gas prices."

I was checking email; Jeff was in the bathroom. Aside from people in Nigeria asking me for money, or others asking if I needed to extend my penis—Jesus, how many people was Julie talking to?—there wasn't much of interest. Except for a message, marked urgent, with the subject line, "Security," from Thanloc_hereweare@gmail.com.

"Grey,

I hope this message finds you well. You came to my home to install a security system. It is working very well; we feel very secure. I have another project for you that I am sure you will accept. I'd like to discuss details with you at your earliest convenience. This is a rather large job, but there is no ceiling to the amount of money you can ask for compensation.

You have my address. Come whenever you are free, but please, as soon as possible. We will be waiting.

Please do not share this message with anyone, and come alone.

Sincerely,
Thanloc

Here we are."

Once I read the salutation, I remembered who Thanloc was. That was about all I understood. But as an American, my interest was piqued once I read there was a job that would pay anything I wanted.

It was at least worth a response.

"Thanloc,

I'm so glad I was of service, and that I helped make you feel more secure. That's our job, and we take it very seriously.

I'd be happy to speak with you in greater detail about this

project. I could come sometime next week, if you're available. Perhaps on Friday, in the afternoon?

Please let me know.

Best,

Grey"

"Man, I don't know how I'm not losing pounds by the day," Jeff said, emerging from the bathroom. "I didn't think it was possible to have so much shit inside of you."

"Oh, it's possible," I said as we got ready to leave. "Just listen to a presidential campaign."

We took the elevator down to the lobby, but stopped after looking through the glass doors. Since the rally hadn't been recognized by the city, no streets were blocked off, and a crowd had clogged the space in front of the building.

"I'm not dealing with that mess," I said.

"Yeah, well what are you going to do?" Jeff asked. "Part the crowd? Have everyone move because you want to get out?"

"How about we slip out the back door?"

"Huh?"

"C'mon, follow me."

I led us through the lobby, around the horseshoe-shaped reception desk, and to the back door that S.T. had asked me to secure.

"Dude, I don't think we should be back here," Jeff said. "Security's really been tightening up lately."

"It's cool, daddy-o," I said. "I am security."

"The alarm's gonna go off!" Jeff yelled. "Are you crazy? I don't even want to know what'll happen then! The freakin SWAT team will probably come after us!"

"Relax," I said. "I installed it. I know how to disarm it."

Though the system looked elaborate, I just reached behind the little box and turned the switch to "off."

"Just remember to turn it back on the next time you're here," I said.

S.T. saw all of this on the camera, positioned above the door. I forgot about this, even though I set it up. He sat riveted, froze the picture, studied it.

He had taken to spending almost all waking hours at home in his office, which was equipped with 15 17-inch monitors. They broadcast nonstop what the miniature video cameras[32] captured. Cameras were:

On mailboxes

In Jumbotrons at sports arenas

In streetlights

In cabs

In traffic lights

On bridges

In the mouths of gargoyles that perched on building ledges

On the internet

On spaceships and satellites

In convenience stores

On and around gas stations

In and around oil refineries

In and around apartment complexes

In, on, and around buildings that housed any government interest, no matter how trivial; this included, but certainly was not limited to, the back door of the PIMBCO building

"It was my job to know what was happening, so the average person could go about his or her daily life without worrying too much. That's why I was chosen for my job. The average person, frankly, doesn't have the mental makeup, the character necessary to worry about protecting people. It's enough to drive a lesser man insane."

—"The Real S.T."

When S.T. saw Jeff and I sneak out the back door, he went nuts. He recognized me as the security installer, which didn't help. Nor did my little fake crouch and criminal dance, done to make Jeff laugh.

He knew who Jeff was, because it was his job "to know who everyone was at PIMBCO."

"So I decided to keep my eye on the security guy. I'd call in a couple of days and bring him back. In the meantime, I'd go have a chat with that Jeff Saltshaker."

—From "The Real S.T."

When I said that S.T. went nuts after seeing us leave the PIMBCO building, I was paraphrasing from what I read in his book. He never said "nuts."

* * *

"Hi there; mind if I come in?"

Jeff looked up from his computer and immediately felt a chilly rumble in his midsection, as if his bowels had ague.

"Uh, yessir," Jeff said. "Are you, um, having any problems with your computer?"

"Not that I know of," S.T. said, closing the door behind him. "But you never can tell these days. There are viruses and trackers so deceptive and clandestine that it's almost impossible to know for sure who's monitoring you."

"That's true," Jeff managed. "That's why we do what we do."

"And that's why we do what we do."

"I'm Jeff Saltshaker," he said, rising to shake hands.

"I know," S.T. said. "I know everybody here. Please; sit down."

Jeff did as he was told. S.T.'s hand wasn't clammy; he always made sure it was dry, and that his shake was firm.

"So Jeff," S.T. said, walking around the office, "how has your workload been? Boss riding you too hard? Making you come in nights, weekends?"

"No," Jeff said, reaching into his pocket for an Immodium. "Things are going great. I mean, we're busy, but I'd rather be busy. Makes the days go by faster." He wiped a bead of sweat from his temple, not realizing that he had an uncapped pen in his hand, leaving a blue streak of ink across the side of his face.

"That's good," S.T. said. He paused when he saw the ink, and, even though Jeff didn't notice anything, S.T. got a little irritated at revealing his surprise. He knew that, like a good poker player, Dylan would have noticed without any tell the ink that wasn't there a second ago. He hated how sometimes, no matter how hard he tried, he felt so transparent, much like high school. His conscience lashed him for his mistake, twenty whips; on some level, he enjoyed this. He silently stared at the corner of the ceiling for almost three minutes, his lips slightly moving.

"Sir," Jeff said, timidly. "Is there anything I can help you with?"

S.T. whirled on Jeff, taking two steps toward him. "What do you know about those who make Decisions? What do you know about the security guy?!"

"Wh-wh-what?" Jeff said, clenching his sphincter.

Just as quickly as he snapped, S.T. harnessed his emotions. He stepped back, took a handkerchief out of his back pocket, and wiped the corners of his mouth at what Jeff hoped was saliva and not foam.

"Well," he said, "I guess I'll let you get back to work. But I want you to know that the most important thing—my goal—is for there to be an open line of communication between every employee here at the PIMBCO building. There is nothing you should feel as though you can't tell me. In fact, we'd prefer you tell us whatever is on your mind. My assistant's door is always open."

He smiled, revealing front teeth streaked with a pink film.

"Have a great day," he said.

As soon as S.T. left, Jeff hobbled to the bathroom. He barely got his pants off (no time to wipe the seat) and started before he even sat down.

"Dude, I'm telling you, it was really fucking freaky," Jeff said to me at Hal's. "So uncomfortable."

"What are you going to do?" I asked.

"What am I going to do? I'm looking for a new job, effectively immediate." He gulped half of his beer, then belched. "I can't work in that environment. You think my stomach was messed up before? I'm gonna have to start wearing a colonoscopy bag if I stay there."

"Man, I can't believe he came to see you. Why are people taking personal interests in everybody that works there?"

"It's the only interest they can take."

"Thank god I'm not there anymore."

"He definitely mentioned you."

"What?!"

"Yeah," Jeff said, stifling a hiccup. "He asked me what I knew about the security guy. How did he even know that I know you?"

"Christ," I said. "He probably saw us sneaking out the back door the other day. I should have known better—I installed the damn cameras!"

"Grrrreat," Jeff slurred, sounding like Tony the Tiger after a stroke. "Well, I'm sure the man is gonna want to talk to—with—talk you. Some point soon."

When I woke up the next morning, a message on my voicemail patiently waited for me.

"Grey, good morning. It's Mr. Youvie from the Department of Energy Security. You did an excellent job installing a system at the PIMBCO building a little while back. We have another little project for you. Hope to hear from you soon. You can call the office; I trust you still have the number on file."

"What do you think I should do?" I asked.

"Stay in bed for another hour," Vivian answered, her voice muffled a bit by the remnants of sleep and my shoulder, which cradled her head.

"That's what I'd like to do," I said, kissing her forehead.

"Then do it."

"I mean about this S.T.," I said, trying to sound nowhere near as nervous as I was. "It's never good when somebody from the government sees you doing something that you shouldn't be doing and wants to talk to you."

"Well, he said it's about business, right? Call him back, ask what he wants, and send somebody else."

It was a great idea, even though I knew that if that worked, time was the only thing it might buy me. When people in power want to talk to people not in power, they force conversation, if necessary.

"Good morning, this is Grey Reflections from Dubs Security Systems returning S.T. Youvie's call. Is he available?"

"One moment, please," the automatron said.

"How are you doing," S.T. said rather than asked. "So glad you called. The project we have for you is one that I'd rather not talk about over the phone. When is the soonest you can get here? If you'd like, a car can pick you up in 15 minutes."

He spoke like an open spigot with a ripped washer, words spouting everywhere.

"That sounds great, Mr. Youvie, and I'm glad that you're pleased with the current system. I'm sure we can accommodate you. Unfortunately, I can't make it today. But I'd be happy to have the office send somebody else—"

"No no no no no," he said. "It has to be you. See, offices like mine…offices that deal with what we deal with…prefer to limit to an absolute minimum the number of guests and outside workers that visit our premises. Since we've already welcomed you, we'll only deal with you. We have a trust, which is not the easiest thing to establish these days."

"I understand, Mr. Youvie, but there's no way I can do it today," I said, pacing. Vivian was in the shower, singing an Arcade Fire song[33]. "If you need it done today, it has to be another of our trusted technicians."

A sigh—not a friendly one—came through the receiver. The voice that followed was cold. "I need you to come in here as soon as possible. How is tomorrow?"

"I don't think tomorrow will work, either."

"Why not?"

"We're starting on a new project that needs all hands on deck."

"What about Thursday?"

"The project is scheduled to take the rest of the week." Sweat coated my ear, making the receiver slick and disgusting.

"Okay," S.T. said, no patience anywhere near his words. "If necessary, I will call your supervisor and tell him that you are needed for an extremely lucrative project. I doubt he will have any problem with that?"

"Probably not," I said.

"By the end of the week. You don't even have to tell me when. Just be here."

"Yes, sir." I said, defeated.

* * *

I called out sick the next two days, which S.T. learned after contacting Dubs. After all, it was his job to know what I was doing.

* * *

The national Energy Rally, the one that had been planned for months, the one that promised to "make a difference," was Saturday. Rallies were scheduled in all of the major cities outside of Texas, with Philly expected to draw as many people as it did for the Live 8 concert in 2005; with none of the bands playing at the rally, it was certain to sound better.

Jeff was officially gooning out at work and living on a BRAT diet[34]. He was so paranoid about his office being bugged, about one day being dragged away in a straitjacket to some Kafka-like island prison, he didn't notice how active in societal issues Celia had become. He didn't even notice that, two weeks before, Celia wrote what she now calls her first blog posting; it appeared on Craigslist's Philadelphia Rants n Raves. The post, seen below, is available on her blog's archives.

"As I watched the season finale of Gossip Girl last night, it hit me, all of a sudden—something needs to be done! There is no way people in this country can

continue living the way we deserve to live if we have to pay so much for necessities like food, gas, and moisturizer. Those things should cost the least so we have more money to spend on luxury items, like education. I made my mind up—I was going to attend the Energy Rally, and I urge that you do as well. If we work as a team, I'm sure we can make a difference!"

She posted the maximum number of pictures of herself (four) with the post, titled "We must do something!!!", which appeared between "Are you feeling pain at the pump?" and "how DARE you say satan will spray his ejaculates on my body!!"

She was instantly deluged with emails, subject lines like, "I hear you loud and clear!", "See you Saturday", "I kno y ou want this big fat cock", and "250 ro$e$ if I can cum on ur feet!!!" She opened every one, and masturbated twice at what she hadn't felt in years—a small semblance of fame.

* * *

I arrived at work on Friday, certain Dubs would ask why I didn't mention the lucrative project at the PIMBCO building. When he didn't, I became even more nervous.

"Have you heard anything over there?" I asked Jeff over the phone.

"What do you mean have I heard anything?" Jeff whispered. "I don't want to hear anything. I don't even want to be here, but I'm more scared of what might go on if I'm not here. I haven't done much aside from look for another job. I've already put in for two weeks vacation, starting Monday. I can't work in this atmosphere. I have a feeling everybody is talking about me and listening to what I'm saying and monitoring my computer activity. It's driving me crazy. Matter of fact, I'm going to start moving some of my stuff out of here tomorrow."

"The rally is tomorrow," I said.

"I know," Jeff said. "I can use a hand—are you busy?"

"Vivian is pretty much making me go to the rally."

"Maybe you'll see Celia down there."

"What? She's going?"

"I know, I can't believe it either. But apparently she's into activism now. I think she got the idea from whatever celebrities are doing with poor kids. I don't know. But she's all about it. She's out shopping for the proper outfit."

To an outsider, Jeff may have seemed paranoid, but the person who was listening to Jeff didn't think that at all.

Some may say that planting a bug in offices and monitoring computer activity is unconstitutional, but those same people are the first ones who'd complain about the government not protecting them if something bad happened. Though I respect wholeheartedly what our founding fathers did, and think of them as nothing less than heroes and legends and geniuses, the Constitution was written hundreds of years ago, during a time when you were lucky enough to have your enemies right in front of you. As we know, the world has since changed. The only way to stop things from happening is by knowing when they'll happen. I mean, the public should have been grateful for the Patriot Act, because all it did was tell people what we had been doing for years. We simply hoped making it public would serve as a deterrent.

It was for the good of the country.

—From "The Real S.T."

Chapter Twenty

Heaven

In the afterlife, nobody complains about the price of gas.

—Peppercorn

I hadn't been sleeping alone much. Vivian and I would alternate in hosting sleepovers. One weekend, though, she had to stay at a farm in Maryland, and I was by myself.

But I did have a visitor.

When I first saw the speck bounding toward me in the dream, I knew who it was. He deftly slowed the racehorse, and was suddenly on an emerald patch of grass, which the horse nibbled.

"Grey, I'd like you to meet Affirmed, last horse to win the Triple Crown."

"Pleased to meet you," I said. The horse looked up, said, "How's it going, buddy?" and resumed munching.

"I'm still waiting for this vision I'm supposed to see."

"Not see," Pepper said, "hear. You'll hear of the vision. But that's not important. What is important is that you believe it."

"Listen to him, neeeiiighhhbor," Affirmed said. "He's a good driver."

"You still can't see what's going to happen?"I asked.

"No. Because a lot of that depends on you. Believe me, the fact that people do have free will is one of the biggest disappointments I've discovered. I thought everything was fated. That way, there'd be n explanation. We'd do what we do because we have to. Turns out you do have some say in the matter. Not much, but some."

"So is this what heaven's like?" I asked.

"What?"

"This. You astride horses all the time. Doing whatever you want."

"What do you think heaven is?"

"I don't know," I said. "Somewhere where nobody wants anything."

"A place where everybody has everything they want?"

"No," I said. "A place where there is no want."

"Would you like to live in a place like that?" he asked.

"Sure, who wouldn't?"

"Just asking." He gently pulled Affirmed's head. "We're off. Remember, believe in the vision. You'll want to."

Chapter Twenty-One

Lamkens Make Their Move

It is time to embrace ourstory.

—Wischa

The Lamkens waited until everything was in place before making their move. They needed to be sure that the men in suits were ensconced in a comfort zone, so much as to let their guard down. It took many years—more than 30—before the carelessness that the Decision Makers were trained to ignore finally settled around them.

The Lamkens also needed to wait until Thanloc had the knowledge, resources and ability to access the super secure hard drive which housed the death ray launch code.

Most importantly, they needed to be sure that their brethren in America found the gray man to secure the island.

"Dearest Thanloc,

I offer tidings of joy. We are delighted to report that everything is set on our end. We hope that you have taken all of the necessary steps to ensure that everything is secure. If this is true, let us know at once, so we can fulfill our destiny.

Here we are.
Wishca"

—Email from Wischa to Thanloc

"Dearest and most respected Elder Wischa,

I accept and caress your tidings of joy. I am delighted to report that everything is set in place on our end. I have met the individual who is to ensure that everything is secure. We have waited a long time, ever since you informed me of my destiny and ourstory, to report this to you.

Soon we will fulfill our destiny.

Here we are.
Thanloc"

—Email response from Thanloc to Wischa

* * *

"I'd like to call this meeting to order," said Mathey III.

The group chuckled as they were served heaping plates of food.

They'd gathered on a Thursday, two days before the Energy Rally, to Decide if anything needed to be done before, during or after.

They didn't seem too concerned. It didn't matter what went on in the world. The Decision Makers lived above the world, detached from it. They stood on the shoulders of everymen, breathing rarified air. They were the horses who defecated all over the road; we got to pick through their shit for something to eat.

Mengith IX spoke first. "I have been around a long time, and have seen crises come and go. This one, though, feels a bit different. I don't know why, and I don't know if it's just me getting on in years, but it feels as if something may come of this. I don't know what, and I don't know what to do about it. Usually, for us, the best action is inaction. Let nature take its course, that sort of thing. We'll be okay in the end. Of that I'm sure."

Nobody said anything, content to eat. Then Maderwood V stood, and the room became still.

"We will do nothing," he said. "We will allow people to rally, because that is what they want to do. And that is all they want to do. They'll accomplish something, and we'll throw them a bone by keeping things stable for, say, the next six months. That will give them plenty of time to forget about it, to move on. It will give them a memory to last a lifetime. When they're old and have grandkids on their knees, or next year, when they play 'Remember when,' they can talk about what their strength and numbers accomplished."

"Sounds great," said Mathey III. "But then why won't they continue to rally, show strength in solidarity, to try and change other things about our country that they find unfair?"

"Because most people do not want to act. They want to live. Acting is taking a chance; anything can happen." He paused; when he resumed speaking, it was with fire. "Do you know why we all sit in this room? Do you know why we make Decisions? Because we ACT! We take chances! We are the ones who grab opportunities by the throat and don't let go! We are the ones who dictate how things will be, because we are the only ones with the balls to do it! The world belongs to those who act, to those who make Decisions, to those who take chances, to those who take people by surprise, to those who mandate that what they say goes. That is why we do what we do. And when we Decide what will happen, that is what happens. You don't get anywhere in this world by sitting on your ass. You don't get anywhere by being subservient. You don't get anywhere by accepting. You get places by demanding, by Deciding, and by never being apologetic."

The room was rapt. Everyone believed him. It was a stirring speech. The effect was exactly what Maderwood V had counted on.

What Maderwood V didn't count on was providing the perfect battle speech for the Lamkens just before they made their move. Churchill could not have done it any better.

The eight Lamken heroes, shrouded in a glow of strength and courage that was not of this world, did not look at each other before taking hold of our destiny. They knew that the moment had arrived, that nothing would stop what was to take place.

They pounced, ocelot-like, quickly disarming the much bigger guards of America, whose instincts, for a brief moment, were intoxicated from the oration of the chief suited man.

Working with surprise and implementing the Lamken ubi[35]*,six heroes swarmed over the American guards as night smothers day, sinking them into unconsciousness.*

The other two heroes went for the chief suited man. The ubi did not bring unconsciousness, but did subdue him. Our other heroes wrangled him to the ground. It was like collaring an aging rhinoceros. Once on the ground he eased, as if he, too, knew of our destiny.

As Wischa had predicted, the other suited men did nothing but watch. They never even moved from their chairs.

—From the Lamken ourstory book "Here We Are"

"Here We Are" is translated into 56 languages, and of course is available in the Lamken library.

It's also on the Lamken web site, www.herewearelamkens.com.

The Lamken heroes who performed the takeover were granted immediate Elder status, even though they all were under 25.

"What the fuck is going on here?" Morsty IV said, without strength. The Decision Makers apparently had Decided to watch their Classified Service agents be bound with hemp twine and bamboo, and muzzled with orange peels. Hollowed out coconut shells were placed on their heads, to simultaneously disorient and relax them when they regained consciousness[36].

More Lamkens entered the room, including Wischa, shuffling like Yoda.

"Listen, we'll give you anything you want," said Mathey III. "Just let us get out of here."

"Ha," scoffed Licious, Wischa's *consigliore*. "You say you can give us anything we want. You cannot give us anything we cannot take for ourselves. We are here to realize our destiny, to fulfill the dream of the great Elder Los. There is nothing you can do to stop destiny."

"What the fuck is your destiny?" asked Morsty IV. "Jesus fucking Christ, is it to kill and eat us or some shit like that? This doesn't even make sense!"

"Our destiny," said Wischa, "is to become the most powerful nation on earth—the most prosperous, the most respected, the most revered. Paradise."

The room again fell silent as the words floated like incense. Then Maderwood V burst out laughing. He was followed by Mathey III and Morsty IV, and soon each Decision Maker was guffawing, except for Mengith IX, who was extremely pale.

"How can you become powerful?" said Mathey III. "Nobody even knows you exist!"

"They soon will," said Wischa.

"How the fuck do you figure that?" asked Morsty IV. "You're using oranges and coconuts as weapons."

"Just because we possess a weapon of awesome power, does not mean we need to use it often," said Wischa. "Or ever."

"And what weapon of awesome power do you possess?" asked Maderwood V.

"A Plasma Death Ray," said Wischa.

Again the group burst into laughter, perhaps because of how ridiculous the weapon sounded when spoken by someone else.

"Well, that's true; I guess you technically are in possession of it," said Maderwood V, no longer laughing. "Or, should I say, this island is where the weapon resides. But we Decide what to do with it."

"Not anymore," said Wischa.

"Oh no?"

"No. Because we soon will possess the code used to activate the weapon. And we have the launch computer, obviously. And we know how to operate it, since we've heard everything that's been said in this room for the past 30 years. And we will be welcomed onto the world market, and we will buy everything we wish because each citizen will be given as much money as he or she desires—thank you very much, by the way, for the money-making machine. We do not wish to hurt anyone, but if we are hurt first, then we will have no choice but to respond with force the world has never seen. After all, it is our destiny."

* * *

The Lamken overthrow of the men in suits was the only recorded act of treachery in their ourstory. Every nation is allowed at least one.

You can't really blame the Decision Makers for letting their guard down in front of the Lamkens. If one is detached from consequence his entire life, you can't possibly expect him to be aware that his words and actions could be used against him. Caution had become more and more alien to the Decision Makers, and it was very difficult to exercise it by flipping a light switch.

> "Dearest and most respected Elder Wischa
>
> With much work, I have been able acquire the first half of the launch code. Understandably, it is a long code, and extremely protected. I should have everything in place by Sunday.
>
> I will await to hear from you regarding our transport home. Needless to say, we all are ready.
>
> Here we are.
> Thanloc."
>
> —*Email from Thanloc to Wischa*

"Dearest Thanloc,

You and your brethren in America will soon be on the soft shores that you no doubt miss so much, though you have never walked on them. The work on our end is complete. When you finish compiling the information, and when you have secured the grey man, we will be ready to fulfill our destiny. But you must act now. We do not have more than 48 hours. I will send details of your transport home.

For now, though, send to me the first half of the code.

Await my word. Fulfill our destiny.

Here we are.
Wischa."

—*Email from Wischa to Thanloc*

Chapter Twenty-Two

Kinetic Energy

When it's raining shit, you better have an umbrella.
—Grey Reflections

After being gouged too long by high gas prices and enduring far too many haughty Prius drivers, the American people finally came together. And organizing a group of millions who have access to the Internet and digital cable and drugs and alcohol and TMZ is no small feat.

New York. Chicago. Boston. Miami. San Francisco. St. Louis. Seattle. Philadelphia. And a lot of other cities without football teams.

I was amazed at how people had used the Internet to actually plan everything.

"It's not like this is something that was just thrown together by a few people in one part of the country," Vivian said at breakfast. "This is organized. We have leaders. We have numbers. Strength. Energy. Most importantly, we have a plan."

"Well, you know what they say," I said. "The best laid plans of mice and men…"

"Yeah?" Vivian asked.

"All go to shit when you implement them. Except for really smart mice, the ones who can get through those mazes. You should see what they can concoct."

* * *

As we emerged from the subway onto Market Street, I felt as though we were on the cusp of something, like the moment just before a sneeze.

At street level, we were met by representatives from Gas-X, handing free samples.

"Don't pay too much for gas! Gas-X helps relieve stress-induced gas bubbles and allows you to sit through meetings without squeezing your cheeks! Free packages! Get your free Gas-X!"

"You sure you don't want any?" I asked Vivian. "Maybe for some of the horses?"

"I think they're okay," she said. She laughed, and grabbed my arm. At that moment, things were good.

Isn't it a shame moments only last for moments?

I called Jeff; he was at his office.

"I've been here since nine," he said. "I can't believe Celia really went to the rally, but she's all about this."

"Is she with you?"

"No. She wanted to walk around, talk to people."

"Do you still need some help packing your stuff?"

"Nah, I should be okay."

"Are you going to march?"

"I highly doubt it," Jeff said. "I caught a glimpse of those Port-a-Potties on my way in, and I'm not getting anywhere near them."

Celia walked the streets, but didn't look for people to talk to. She was more interested in finding where the television cameras were, so she'd know where to stand. She'd prepared some comments in case she was interviewed.

She also prepared her outfit, which came from a magazine more than a closet, in case she was interviewed. Simple black tahan skirt suit with classic black peep-toes, their red soles flashing with each step. Black sunglasses on her head, holding back her hair, more accessory than necessity.

She'd even brought a small notepad and pen, in case she wanted to take notes for her postings on Twitter.

S.T. watched from his office in the PIMBCO building everything that his micro-video cameras, overlooking the streets, broadcast. He could zoom in so close as to know which people shaved their private areas; not that he would ever do that—he just wanted his cameras to have the most high-powered zooms in case somebody tried to use a mini-bomb.

Whenever there are large gatherings, no matter the country, the possibility of civil disobedience arises. All it takes is one person to yell 'fire!' in a theater for pandemonium to break out. But the beauty of America is that the government cannot stop people from demonstrating, or gathering, or expressing their opinions. All we can do is arrest those who do.

Again, I must stress that I did not premeditatedly scout the rally to make any arrests. But since I was looking to speak with Mr. Reflections, and he was not returning my phone calls, and I knew that he would be in attendance, I figured I'd run into him, and we could have a friendly, informative, chat.

After all, I was simply doing my job. And believe me, you are very glad that I did it well.

—From "The Real S.T."

* * *

"So what are these things usually like?" Rookie Officer Tommy Briddes asked Nine-rally Veteran Steven Malone. The two were stationed in front of City Hall, the mayor deploying—by federal order—more than half of the city's police officers in and around Center City. S.T. took credit for the calm that the rallies in his quadrant had thus far maintained, contending that nothing deters citizens from acting out more than men in uniforms with weapons.

Unfortunately for S.T., his plan backfired. With so much police at the rallies, fewer were at gas stations around hits cities. This resulted in several shoot-outs between owners and people who peeled out without paying. S.T. had anticipated that possibility, but also knew he couldn't make an omelet without breaking a few eggs.

"Well, that depends on the rallyers," Malone answered. He looked at Briddes and smiled. "We react to them. Don't worry—follow my lead. With so many of us here, nothing's going to happen. Our presence is enough to scare most of them into submission."

"You don't buckle your chinstrap?"

"Nah. I like to have it loose. Try it; it'll stay on the ol' noggin." Briddes unbuckled the chinstrap. His head was still snug.

* * *

The crowd was immense. Vivian and I hung around the fringe. I didn't want to be walled in among the people, many of whom looked—and smelled—as if they were practicing serious conservation methods when it came to bathing. Vivian didn't want to get "boxed in," like the best horse in the Derby who can't make his move because of the all of the congestion around him.

What we didn't realize is that our hanging around the outskirts of the crowd also made us much easier to spot for S.T., and anybody else who wanted to find us.

I perched on the 22nd floor of the PIMBOC building with two laptops, binoculars, and a high-powered telescope, monitoring the actions of the crowd. I tried communicating with my colleagues in other cities, but couldn't get through to anyone. That was not uncommon; I was often the only member of our team that worked, shall we say, diligently.

I had, directly caused by my dedication, an ulcer the size of a lady's bowling ball. I was swigging three bottles of Maalox and Pink Bismuth a day. And people still criticize how I did my job!

My surveillance team included eight plainclothes officers, positioned randomly among the crowd. It didn't take me long to zero in on the person I was looking for.

I alerted my octet to wait for my signal.

—From "The Real S.T."

S.T. may have seen but paid no attention to four copper-skinned youths. They fit in with everyone else, communicating to each other on cell phones, and positioned themselves at the north, south, east and west sides of the rallyers. Their sole purpose was to look for me; Thanloc was the only one who had ever met me, but the others had seen pictures, and had no doubt that they would find me. After all, they were meant to.

The plan was to march from 30th Street Station, which really was 24th Street, down Market Street until they reached City Hall at 14th, where a stage was set up. Five speakers were scheduled to address the crowd, including actor and local celebrity Peter Patrikios and Bumper Lovin'; three large video screens were erected to broadcast a documentary on alternative forms of energy and a 10-minute film, *Stewed Time*, by local filmmaker Desire Malone, based on the Doc Fillippo story[37].

Marchers marched, linked arm in arm.

Some toted empty gas cans.

Some had fake gas pumps sticking out of their asses.

Some dressed in fatigues.

Some wore flip-flops.

Old, young, black, white, Asian.

Some held signs about the president.

Some carried signs that were misspelled.

Some chanted through bullhorns.

Step by step.

Step by step.

Step by step.

Zeitgeist crackled through the crowd.

I squeezed Vivian's hand.

She smiled at me.

"No longer will we cave to the corporate appetite!"

"No longer will we line the pockets of billionaire barons!"

When we shouted these lines, we believed them.

At least I did.

"And this is just Philly!" Vivian said. "Imagine what is happening in other major cities!"

The only problem was, nobody knew when to stop. With thousands heading toward City Hall, it was easy for the ones up front to stop when they reached Billy Penn. Those farther back, who couldn't see the stage, never ceased coming.

And the inertia was awesome.

Before the people in front knew what happened, the back wave overtook them, tumbling them onto police, who were like pawns on a chess board.

Once surrounded, police reacted with riot gear and mace. A sprayed protestor swung his fists, punching a police horse in the mouth. The horse jerked its head, turned and kicked out a hind foot, hitting in the small of her back a 19-year old girl holding a clarinet, knocking out four of her front teeth. Now-out-of-control protestors saw the girl on the ground and converged around the police; projectiles from the middle of the pack landed all around. Some marchers scurried about, trying to get everybody in order; peaceful people ran away.

Rookie Officer Briddes was at this point separated from Nine-Rally Veteran Malone. He whirled left and right, extinguishing as many fires as he could, hoping this was just a big misunderstanding.

Police chopped through the crowd with batons as if going through a jungle with machetes. When they reached a smaller individual who couldn't conceal fear, they threw him or her up against the nearest car or wall and handcuffed, frisked, copped a feel.

Protestors who fought back did so like *mujaheddin*, run-by random attacks, not necessarily caring about who or what or why they attacked.

The most confused were, without a doubt, the police horses. They couldn't understand why certain people attacked them, why they were yanked one way or another by their riders. The whinnied their irritation, but as usual, nobody listened, nor understood.

Even on the fringe, Vivian and I got jostled around. I took an elbow to the face, bloodying my nose. Vivian ducked and weaved like Sugar Ray Leonard, avoiding flailing limbs. We held hands the entire time, so even when I couldn't see her, we were together. I tried screaming to her, but nothing was heard over the noise, which no longer came from anywhere in particular, and just was.

Once things got out of hand, the speakers tried addressing the crowd, but began yelling over who should go first, and started fighting. *Stewed Time* was aired, but I don't think anyone saw it.

I saw that something needed to be done. I took action.

"We've got to get out of here!" I yelled.

Seeing how much help I was, Vivian sidled over to a horse and spoke into its ear. The horse was jittery, and jerked back its head, not wanting to listen. Vivian soothingly stroked the horse's neck. It finally calmed down, and she leaned in and whispered once again. The horse whinnied. If I didn't know any better, I would have sworn it was laughing.

"C'mon," Vivian called to me. "Hop on."

"What do you mean, hop on?" I ask. "How am I supposed to hop on? I've never hopped on before."

"Just put your foot here and swing your leg over. I'll help you."

I surprised myself with how smooth my mount was. As we rode off,

Vivian guided the horse in and out of crazed gas-crisis rallyers like a gold-medal slalom skier. I couldn't believe that a few moments earlier, this animal was acting like one of the crazed gas-crisis rallyers.

"How did you get the horse to calm down?" I asked.

"I opened with a joke," she said.

How do I know what the officers said to each other, and everything else that went on? The made-for-television movie, *Kinetic Energy*, starring Patrikios, which aired to astronomical ratings and, I'm sure, made its sponsors very happy.

And what was S.T. doing? Following me.

Once I spotted the suspect, I immediately pursued. The problem the crowd kept pushing me back, wave after wave of people knocking me further and further away.

It was quite a metaphor regarding my position in trying to adequately secure America while facing so much criticism and resistance from the general public.

—From "The Real S.T."

During the commotion, a newswoman on the scene committed the unforgivable sin of leaving her post while news happened all around her. The cameraman, in a freakish accident, got hit in the head with a police baton (not intentionally, I hope), and dropped his camera. There lay a news microphone and camera, operating, filming, recording. The eternal question of if nobody stands in front of a camera, does it record? was answered, as Celia, positioned by fate, stumbled across them.

When the camera's sensual red light made eye contact, her heart caromed wildly against her chest. She instinctively picked up the microphone, propped the camera against a nearby wall so that the action in the street was her backdrop, and got to work.

Checking her reflection in the mirror, she took a deep breath.

"Hello, this is Celia Lacey for FOX29 news. I'm here live at City Hall, on the scene of a rally that has turned chaotic. People are running around, and the noise and flying debris are simply too much for the senses to handle. It seems as if the city's population has exploded in a frenzy of emotions and fear." Brushing aside the wisps of dyed blonde hair that waved in front of her eyes, Celia motioned behind her—never looking away from the camera, so as not to ruin the personal connection with the viewer—every few seconds to make sure people knew when to take their eyes off her and look at what she was reporting. When she said, "The peaceful march has now turned into what looks like a bloody and brutal mess of frustrations, emotions, and revolution," there were traces of fear in her voice, though the quavering could have been exhilaration.

"We're trying to talk to some of the people.... Let me see if I can grab somebody.... Excuse me, excuse me, sir, could I ask you a few questions?" Celia approached a middle-aged man running by. As soon as he saw a pretty woman with a microphone, he stopped in his tracks.

"Hi," he said.

"Hello. I'm Celia Lacey from FOX29 News, and we're here with..."

"John Mabrey."

"...John Mabrey, who is among the people seemingly running for their lives. Could you tell us what is going on, from your point of view?"

"Well, I was walking down Broad Street about an hour ago, and all of a sudden things got crazy. There was noise, people yelling and running, cars crashing and things falling from the sky." Mabrey's voice was completely level, and he didn't seem nervous at all, as even he knew he was on camera and should therefore act appropriately.

"Wow, you were just walking when all of this happened. So now where are you headed?"

"Well, I think I'm going to try and get home, make sure my family's okay. If you're watching, hi guys! I'll be home soon."

"John, thank you so much," Celia said, shaking his hand and returning to the camera. Just as she did this, a van screeched beside her, startling her. Two FOX29 news men popped out.

"Oh, I'm sorry," Celia said, backing away but holding onto the mic. "I didn't mean—"

"Are you kidding?" the passenger side man said. "You were great." He had on a FOX29 News jacket and hair that didn't move despite the wind. "We ran what you did. We watched it in the van on the way over. You've got natural talent, girl. And since you were the only newscaster here that didn't get trampled, we must have killed on the ratings."

"Oh my gosh, really?" Celia smiled and turned toward the camera.

"Yeah," the driver said. "Why don't you take a ride with us, come downtown, so we can talk a little business?"

"That would be...wow, sure."

"Okay, hop in."

"What about the cameraman?" Celia asked.

"Oh him?" the passenger said, climbing in after her. "We called the paramedics, told them where he was. They'll be here soon, I'm sure. They'll take care of him."

"Wow, I can't believe this. This is great. I'm Celia Lacey."

"We heard."

* * *

Other cities faced similar consequences as a result of the rallies.

The New York crowd went nuts due to the free handouts from Gas-X. Shouting "Make it rain!" and "Give me my money!", groups of rallyers (and pedestrians) surrounded the representatives, who were distributing gift certificates from five to 25 dollars. The representatives, who were not trained in how to handle a zealous mob, tried their best to get out of the mob's clutches. Some of the rallyers then tried organizing a hasty march against Gas-X, but it didn't take, and the afternoon, though planned with good intentions, didn't produce the outcome many had hoped for.

In Boston, people received free iced tea, but it was unsweetened, and got dumped into the harbor.

Rallyers in Kansas City, Kansas fueded with leaders from Kansas City, Missouri.

* * *

As we made our way to 30th Street Station, I reached for my phone to call Jeff.

"I don't have my phone," I said.

"Where is it?" Vivian asked.

"I don't know. I must have dropped it."

"Let me call it, see if we hear it ring."

She called. We heard nothing. My cell phone was gone.

What a drag.

"Well, forget about it," she said. "You'll have to get a new one."

We dismounted, and were about to make our way to the train when I saw heading our way two other horses, each carrying two copper-skinned people. They rode up Market Street shrouded with auras, almost like haloes—though it could have been the sun reflecting off of the glass and steel of buildings and cars.

For whatever reason, I was completely at ease the entire time these horses neared. They were about 10 yards away when I saw that one of them was Thanloc.

"You must come with us," Thanloc says. "You will help fulfill our destiny."

"WHAT?"

"You are to secure our future."

Whoa. I wasn't expecting that.

"Grey, you are to secure our island, and play an instrumental role in Lamken becoming New Utopia."

"Who is this?" Vivian asked. "And what the hell is he talking about?"

"I don't know," I said. "I mean, I know who he is. He's a customer.... But I don't know...dude, really, what in God's name are you talking about?"

"You are a crucial part of ourstory," Thanloc said. "You were seen in the vision by the great Elder, Los, when he was stranded on the side of Mount Laddis many years ago. You are to come with us to Lamken as we become the most powerful and richest nation in the world."

"Okay, look, it was great seeing you again," I said. "But we're late on our way to reality. Tell you—"

I stopped. "What did you say about vision?"

"That's right, man." I turned and saw another figure on a horse. "I know it sounds crazy, but everything he's saying is true," Peppercorn said.

"Don't fuck with me, man," I said. "Seriously. I don't need that right now. I just lost my phone, the rally is out of control. This is all too much."

"I'm serious," Peppercorn said. "Remember when I said I could only see a few pages ahead? Well, you better go with these guys right now. Talk to them. Or, hear them out. What they'll tell you, you'll see things that prove what they are saying is true. You shouldn't go home. It's not safe for you."

"This is beyond insanity," I said. "You're telling me, in all seriousness, to go with these people right now, on a horse, instead of hopping on a train with my girlfriend?"

"Grey, who the fuck are you talking to?" Vivian asked. "You're really starting to freak me out."

I just realized I was having a conversation with a dead person in the company of my live girlfriend. If anything, that taught me that live girlfriends—who are sane—won't find it attractive if you speak out loud to dead people.

Then I looked over at Thanloc and saw that he, too, appeared to be engaged in a conversation with the air directly to his left.

"Listen," Peppercorn said. "Do you trust me? Have you ever trusted me?"

"Yeah, all the time," I said. "That's why it was always so easy for you to break my balls."

"Well, I swear to you, that no matter how bizarre and crazy it sounds, you have to go with these guys right now. Listen to them. Then make up your mind and do whatever you want. But go with them now. And fast. You don't have much time."

"I just can't leave," I said. "What about Vivian?"

"I'm sorry, man," he said.

"What about me?" she asked. "I think I'm the only one here on this planet. And I'm getting out of here. On a train. If you're coming with me, let's go. If not, goodbye." She said that with tears in her eyes. I think she knew it was over. No matter what I said.

"You're leaving me," I said.

"Right now, I'm getting on a train," she said. "And I'm going home. And tomorrow I'm going to work. Tonight I hope to speak to you. So call me."

Then she kissed me, ducked into the station, and rolled down the track.

Though I don't know exactly who the apparition was that Thanloc was speaking to, I did find out why he saw what he saw.

All Lamken children spoke with apparitions of Lamken Elders long deceased. They never questioned why they saw these things; they thought it was normal.

On Lamken, everyone chews a dried leaf called *bissleliscious wakan*, that, loosely translated, means rub-a-dub-delly-all-in-my-belly. The leaf produces a tremendously soothing effect, as much kick as a double espresso, and, depending on how much you eat, hallucinations.

I enjoy it in small doses, though even those at first made me a little nauseous. Then I thought of what Peppercorn once said: "When in Rome, chew *bisslelisciouswakan*."

Here we are.

Chapter Twenty-Three

One Helluva Hacker

The security breach of my personal computer, hacked through the most sophisticated software protection known to man, is a prime example of why the government needs to know what people are doing with their computers.

—"The Real S.T."

Nobody spoke in the car[38] on the way to Thanloc's house. I was in no mood to talk, in that I felt that all of my free will had left the building, that I was no longer in control of what happened to me.

It was a helpless feeling.

We stopped at Thanloc's house. He got out, and I wordlessly followed. When we walked in the front door, his mother, like so many others, doted on us.

"Can I get you something to eat?" she asked. "To drink? A cool washcloth for your forehead? You must be hungry. After all, fulfilling a destiny is exhausting."

"I'm fine, mom," Thanloc said.

"Well, what about Mr. Grey?"

"I, uh, I think I'm okay for right now," I said.

"I'll fix you a glass of coconut milk," she said. "Nobody can resist my coconut milk."

"Okay, mom," Thanloc said, with a perfect mix of exasperation, love and respect that American young adults have mastered. Or, at least, used to have mastered. "Let's go downstairs," he said. "I'd like to show you something."

When I got down to the basement, I stopped. I couldn't believe what I saw.

Computers and monitors lined one entire wall. There had to be more than 10 monitors, and I don't even know how many computers, because the entire lower part of the wall looked like one giant hard drive. Things whirred and beeped while screen savers danced, funneled, and did lava-lamp shit. Since I've never seen a NASA office, it was safe for me to say that this is what a NASA office would have looked like.

He sat down at a desk and hit a button. The monitor changed to what I assumed was a live shot of the outside of my apartment. His fingers worked some kind of a joystick that rotated the view, zoomed in and out. He positioned the shot so it was looking in my window, then zoomed in so far as to show my cat sleeping.

"What the fuck is this shit?" I asked.

"This is your apartment," he said.

"I'm aware. Why are you watching me? How long have you been spying on me? What the fuck is wrong with you people?"

"We are not spying on you," Thanloc said. "In fact, we only set these cameras up this morning, to show you what would happen."

"Which is what?"

"We'll have to wait and see," he said.

"I have coconut milk!" Thanloc's mother called.

The coconut milk was out of this world.

I didn't have my cell phone, so I couldn't talk to anyone. I mean, I couldn't even call from a land line or pay phone, because I didn't know anybody's number. My cell phone memorized them for me.

Thanloc told me to make myself at home, watch television, read, or play a computer game. "Just don't check your email," he said. "Because that could be traced to here."

He started typing furiously, with speed that the roadrunner would have envied, if the roadrunner could have typed. Soon, the monitor he was working on was covered with numbers and letters that constantly changed.

"What are you doing?" I asked. "Creating the matrix?"

"Downloading a code."

"For what?"

"A weapon."

"What kind of weapon?"

"Plasma Death Ray."

"Plasma *what*?"

"Plasma Death Ray," he said without taking his eyes off of the screen. "I know, it's a ridiculous name. But it exists. The launch code is a few pages long. I've got the first half of it, but, as you would imagine, it is behind anti-hacker security software the likes of which you couldn't even imagine. So it's taking me a long time."

"How long have you been trying to get the code?"

"A couple of months."

"Where are you trying to get it from? The government?"

"Something like that," he said. "Though it's not a government computer. It's actually a personal computer."

Now, I know what you may be thinking: that I was in way too calm a state to have had this conversation with Thanloc at this time. The best explanation as to how I was able to maintain myself, I guess, would be that uncertainty principle I'd mentioned to Julie a while back, which said that you couldn't judge the speed and location of something at the same time. So as long as I was in this conversation, I couldn't see how ludicrous it really was.

Or something like that.

It had indeed taken Thanloc months to hack through the security walls in Dylan's computer—after weeks of hacking through S.T.'s computer to get to Dylan's—being surgically precise not to trip any alarm, which he so artfully anethesitized in his cyber way.

Over the next couple of hours, I drank coconut milk and played some retro Castelvania[39] on the computer. All of the computer equipment in the basement, which allowed Thanloc to hack into pretty much anything he wanted, cost well over a couple of million dollars. Funds were no problem, as the Lamkens had for decades sent money him the necessary funding. Most of the computers were without brand names; Thanloc had put them together with parts purchased at computer conventions.

As if the money sent from Lamken wasn't enough, Thanloc had hacked onto online poker sites and made hundreds of thousands of dollars off of programs that allowed him to see his opponents' cards as well as which cards were yet to come[40]. He did this for shits and wiggles[41].

Around seven o'clock, the camera trained on my apartment showed four people knock on my front door. Then it showed those same people breaking in.

"Jesus Christ!" I said. "What are they doing?! Zoom in, get the camera back inside!"

Thanloc wheeled over in his chair, took control of the joystick, positioned the camera to zoom and follow the men. Althea hissed and scampered under the bed as they opened drawers and checked closets. One of the men unplugged my computer and carried it out. After about a half-hour, they left.

"Oh my god," I said. "I'm in serious trouble."

"That is why you were not safe there," Thanloc said, matter of factly. "That is why you should stay here."

"Stay here? For how long?"

"It won't be long. Once we have word, we will return to Lamken."

"Return to *what*?! What are you talking about? I'm not going anywhere. I'm staying here, in this country, in this town, in this state, with the people I know, and with my job, and with my cat. I'll probably have to get another apartment, but otherwise I intend to go back to living my life the way it was, possibly without my girlfriend—who I couldn't blame at all for leaving me after all of this weird shit—but I will be back to living the life I had before today!"

"That is not your destiny," Thanloc said. "Your destiny is to come with us, and to secure our island, as we ascend to New Utopia."

"Whatever you say, buddy," I said. "I'm getting out of here."

"But where will you go?" he asked. "You cannot go home. They are still waiting for you to arrive. If you don't believe me, look." He pulled the camera back from the inside of my house to a van across the street. He zoomed in on the van, and I was surprised to see the camera film *through the sides* to show two agent-looking people sitting on what I gathered to be two really comfortable chairs. "Do you think they are plumbers, on call?"

I said nothing, utterly confused and defeated.

"It didn't matter if those people were there, or if anyone was after you," he said. "You must realize that one cannot change his destiny. The path that has been laid out for you is the only one you can travel. And paths are not laid out for everyone. There are many people in the world that have none. Those are the ones who wander aimlessly. There is no telling what they have to live for. And those people are not to be blamed. They cannot help the fact that no path was laid for them. They can only live their lives the way they choose.

"But the ones who have a destiny, who have a path shaped for them long before they were ever born, are the ones who must follow that. It is inexcusable for them not to. Oftentimes, that path is not easy. But it will always reap the biggest reward, because that is the way it was meant to be."

Here we are.

Then, as if things couldn't have gotten any more Twilight Zone-y, I appeared on television. Every local station. NBC10. 6ABC. KYW3. FOX29. On the news. As a fugitive. Which was made all the more strange considering I didn't remember being charged with a crime. Any persons with knowledge of my whereabouts should immediately contact not the local police, but the Department of Energy Security.

Some people wait their entire lives to be on tv. I didn't know how I should have reacted.

Mr. Reflections was a fugitive because he fled an attempted arrest. During the rally, I yelled at him to stop, but he continued, resisting arrest by fleeing. So I decided to place him on the fugitives list, in order to stop any additional illegal activity in which he was participating.

Of course, it turns out I was right, because he was in the group who hacked into Dylan Maderwood V's personal computer through my computer to steal highly sensitive information regarding the protection of the United States of America. Sometimes, you wish you weren't right.

—From "The Real S.T."

The van outside of my apartment left a little after midnight. Thanloc and I were awake; he was still working on the launch code.

"I think we should return to your apartment now," he said, "so you can gather anything you need."

When we arrived at my apartment, Thanloc and his cousins kept watch outside. Althea asked what was for dinner.

Chapter Twenty-Four

By the Balls

Are these fucking mutherfuckers kidding me?
—Dennis Mathey III, shortly after the Lamken takeover

It was early, the sun itself with only one foot out of bed. I couldn't sleep. Aside from the time spent at my apartment gathering my things, Thanloc worked nonstop trying to download the rest of the launch code. He had incredible concentration and discipline. It surprised me that he could work for so long without coffee or Red Bull. He chewed *bissileliciouswakan*, though at that point I didn't know that's what it was.

I'd brought two small suitcases of clothes, Althea, my photo album, passport, and some CDs with me to Thanloc's. I only packed for a couple of days, weeks at the most. I still didn't believe what Thanloc said, but did realize that powerful people were chasing me[42].

"You're still not finished?" I asked.

"It's very well protected," Thanloc said. "But I almost have it."

"What will you do when you finish getting the code?" I asked.

"Send it to Wischa."

"What happens if somebody finds out that you're trying to get the code?"

"They won't."

"How do you know?" I asked.

"Because they can't. This is part of our destiny."

"But what if somebody does? Like you told me, what if somebody doesn't follow their destiny, and breaks up your destiny? What then?"

"Then we wait to hear word from Wischa."

"Who is this Wischa? Where is he? What is he doing while you're risking your life to get this code?"

* * *

"Are you all comfortable?" Wischa asked. "Is there anything we can get you? After all, we are here to serve you."

It had been almost 24 hours since the Lamken coup. The Classified Service agents remained tightly bound and under careful watch. The Decision Makers, part of a situation which couldn't possibly have been more alien to them, didn't know what to do.

"Oh, I don't think my stomach is in any shape to eat anything," said Mengith IX. "Perhaps some fruit, and a café latte with skim milk. And some toast. But nothing more."

"It has been a day," Maderwood V, the only Decision Maker who seemed to have any life in him, said, "and we have not yet seen the rest of the launch code. I hope, for your sake, that you have not placed too much confidence in your young people."

"You will see it shortly. First, I'd like to negotiate our demands."

"Fuck your demands!" Mathey III said. "And let us out of here! If you know what's good for you."

"Please try and control yourselves," Wischa said. "You'll be home soon. But not until we come to an agreement."

"Okay," Maderwood V said. "What is it you want?"

"The four women, who had been traded for the money-making machine, are to be returned without harm to the island," said Wischa. "They will be accompanied by their children and one American. If any of them are even the slightest bit harmed, we will fire the Plasma Death Ray at the American cities in which all of you reside."

"If all you wanted was the women, children, and one American," said Maderwood V, "this little takeover, or whatever you'd like to call it, was not necessary."

"Perhaps it was not necessary," said Wischa. "You can call it an insurance policy. For our next demand."

"Which is?" asked Maderwood V.

"That Lamken be officially recognized as a nation, and introduced to the global marketplace. We have had, for years, the financial resources. Now we have the military resource as well."

"This is ridiculous," said Morsty IV. "You don't have any military resources. You have half of a code to launch a weapon that you most likely don't even know how to control." He turned to Dylan. "I think we've been giving these people a little too much credit. They don't have the entire code. They can't do anything with what they have. And even if they had it, they don't know how to aim the Death Ray. And now they're making demands? They want to join the global marketplace? We can't allow that. Everyone will know about them. We'll have to find another place to meet!"

"Perhaps we don't know exactly how to operate the sun weapon," said Wischa. "Perhaps we'll have to learn how to properly control it. That might take a few trials. Target practice, if you will. You must understand that we do not wish to harm anyone. But we understand that the power of this weapon is the only thing that will speed up negotiations."

Wischa turned his gaze on Maderwood V, who said, "Your demands are not unreasonable. But you have not yet shown that you have the launch code. Without that, negotiations will, in all likelihood, be altered."

"Then I guess it's time to, as you say, turn our cards over?" Wischa asked with a smile.

"Got it!" Thanloc exclaimed. "Destiny, here we come."

He sent the rest of the launch code to Wischa. In this century, destinies cannot possibly be fulfilled without an "enter" key and a "send" button.

When Wischa displayed on the giant screen the entire launch code, the Decision Makers reacted thusly:

Donald Mengith IX let out a little gasp.

Dennis Mathey III cursed.

David Morsty IV forced a whimper.

Duncan Manow uttered a wow.

Dylan Maderwood V showed no emotion.

For with the code to the Plasma Death Ray, this tiny island nation had America and the Decision Makers exactly where the Decision Makers and America had so many other nations for so so long.

By the balls.

Once in that grip, the Decision Makers felt something very unfamiliar to them.

Defeat.

Here we are.

Chapter Twenty-Five

Let's Go

Let's go.
—Dylan Maderwood V

We received word from Wischa that two helicopters would meet the eight Lamkens and one American[43] at a field in Kennett Square[44], about 30 minutes south of Philadelphia. Me, Thanloc, and the three younger Lamkens—Ptash, Scudseman, and Drizzle—and Althea in one car, the adult women in the other, drove down Route 1 until we reached Chester County.

We arrived at the field at dusk. The Lamkens had rested during the day, while I repeatedly called the track in search of Vivian. I left messages. She never called back.

What can you do?

I did, however, hear several more bulletins about my being wanted.

With my options limiting—and with Kennett Square drawing nearer by the second—I reached into my wallet, pulled out my business card, asked Thanloc to borrow his cell phone, and called Dubs' direct line.

"Dubs here."

"It's Grey."

"Grey!" he said. "Where are you? I'bbe been trying to contact you all day!"

"What's the matter with you?" I asked. "Why are you talking like that?"

"Oh. I just got back from the dentist. I'm all full of nobacaine."

"Jesus, I can hardly understand you."

"Nebber mind that," he said. "Why am I seeing you on telebision as a wanted criminal? What habe you gotten yourselb into? I don't eben belieebe it!"

"I have to ask you for a really big favor," I said. "Is there any way you could meet me in Kennett Square? I lost my phone, and don't really know if I can go home, and I really need to talk to Jeff."

"Sure, I can meet you," he said. "Where?"

"In a field just off of Route 1 by Gatemaster's General Store."

"Okay, Gatemaster's General Store. I will be there in a half-hour."

"Thanks man."

I thought Dubs was being a good guy. What I didn't know was that S.T. had promised Dubs a reward if he could help bring me in[45].

"You are thinking of not coming with us?" Thanloc asked.

"I'm thinking about doing what's best for me."

"You cannot escape your destiny," he said. "Haven't you read Greek drama? Or seen Star Wars?"

We made our way through Kennett. The foul, pungent smell of mushrooms growing in shit punched us in the face, made us roll up the windows. There were rolling hills, fields, and a horizon that changed depending on which way you looked and which road you were on.

The general store was closed by the time we got there, just after dusk. Ours were the only cars. Although it wasn't as if we were in Montana or anything, to me this was the country. And it felt like the country. Not desolate or anything; just still.

"So now what?" I ask.

"We wait," Thanloc said.

"You know, this fulfilling your destiny stuff seems to be filled with a lot of waiting around. Isn't here like a speed-up plan or something?"

Nobody laughed.

We waited about an hour. Why was Dubs taking so long? He should have been here 20 minutes ago.

It was at this moment that I decided to take off. I didn't know how far I'd get or where I'd go or how fast I'd be able to move with a cat in a carrier. But I figured to do what these people had said they were doing, and take my destiny into my own hands. I'd get myself a lawyer, and get out of the wrongful charges against me, because I was innocent, and in America you didn't get punished for things you didn't do[46].

Just as I was about to take my first step, four black cars drove up the undulating road. Fast.

The Lamkens became excited, holding hands and saying, "Here we are." I didn't like the looks of it. It didn't feel right, just as black cars driving toward you—fast—almost never feels right.

Tires chirped to a halt and men poured out. Suits. Uniforms. Guns.

There was no way I could have outrun them. Well, maybe S.T., but never the other members of his posse.

Honestly, I don't even remember if I ran at all. There were on me so quickly, I about shit my pants.

In a blink I was face down, a powerful knee in my back, at least two guns pointed on my head, my feet and hands cuffed.

"I want him alive!" I heard. "I want him alive!"

It seemed like a long time before S.T. came huffing and puffing. It seemed an even longer time before he caught his breath and straightened up. Then he bent down and put his face in mine.

"I won't even lie," he said, his breath reeking of antacids and the edges of his lips crusted pink. "This is the highlight of my career. Having you in this position, you thief of energy and security, almost makes what you did worth it. We are going to have long talks, you and I—and your friends over here, too. Oh, the tales we'll tell. The tears you'll cry. I can promise you this—when we get through with you, you'll never hack into another computer again."

"Hack?" I asked. "I'm not a hacker! Those guys were the hackers! I never hacked into anything!" Obviously, I had no loyalty, and was not in the slightest afraid to squeal like a nerdy first-grader about Thanloc and his friends.

"Then why are you with them?" he asked. "Why have you been avoiding me? Why did you flee the rally when I attempted to arrest you?"

Those questions I couldn't answer. I cried instead.

I looked over and saw the Lamkens being handcuffed without resistance. They all sat cross-legged on the ground. They seemed so calm. They looked like Buddhists.

"What you stole from us," he said, "you will never use. We won't let you. But what I really want to know is why you would want to hurt this great country? Has it not provided you with everything you need?"

"What?" I asked. "Sure, yeah."

"Then why do you want to incinerate parts of it?"

"What? I don't! What the hell are you talking about?"

"I don't expect you to say much," he said. "But after a few months at one of our questioning facilities, perhaps you and your friends here will say a bit more. I haven't quite figured out where to send you yet…."

Althea hissed at the man who lifted her crate.

And then cameth the man. Mr. Dylan Maderwood V.

When he arrived, it wasn't 20 people in uniforms with guns taking positions behind mailboxes and rooftops.

He was there, like oxygen.

I didn't even hear the helicopters land. But there were four of them, sitting on the field like giant metal insects.

He didn't need an army. All he needed was to stride up, look down, block out the sun, and look from behind his glasses, which weren't tinted.

"Look what I did, Dad!" S.T. said. "I got him! I got all of them!"

"Let them go," Maderwood V said, nodding slightly to the Lamken-Americans. One of his people went over and, with something that he pulled from his pocket, uncuffed all of them.

"Wait," S.T. said, though nobody listened.

"You are the grey man, I presume," Maderwood V said to me.

"I am the grey man?" I asked.

"Let me ask, then," he said. "Are you the grey man?"

"That's my name, yeah."

"Uncuff him," he said. In seconds my wrists were free. I didn't dare stand, though.

"You have a choice. You can go with these people," he said, gesturing to Thanloc and the Lamkens, "or you can go with these people," he said, gesturing to S.T. and his crew. "Those are your options. You have 30 seconds to decide. If you can't decide by then, a Decision will be made for you. Your fate is up to you."

Seemed like an easy choice, huh? Looking back on it, it was. But my mind didn't know what to think at that point. I didn't know who any of these people around me were. I had no clue where Thanloc and the others were heading. But door number two was bad—that I knew. I figured I was going to Gitmo or to some prison with Abu in the title. And that I surely didn't want.

Then, maybe to help me make up my mind, Peppercorn appeared. He didn't stop, like all the other times. The horse he was on galloped by. I even felt the hoofs pounding the ground, which I thought was really weird, because if he was just an apparition, how could he make any physical effect?

At any rate, he called out, "Take the gamble, man. No risk, no reward. Take the shottttttttttttt," his voice fading as he rode off.

I didn't say anything. I just pointed to Thanloc.

We boarded two large helicopters. I thought for a second that we would be shot and killed, or taken straight to jail. But we weren't. We were flown to what I can only imagine was a private airport, where we got in a jet that was like the Ritz Carlton.

I sat next to Thanloc. I asked how he kept so calm during the arrest, hoping to hear some Jedi-like mind trick in which you can center all of your energy and block out everything around you.

"Destiny," he said. "You can't stop it."

Letting the arrested parties go that evening was the most painful moment of my career. Though I of course didn't argue with Dylan's decision, I didn't necessarily agree with it either. The parties were guilty of endangering American lives, and they should have been punished for it, not sent off to some island paradise simply because their leaders demanded it. We worked for the government of the United States of America. The best interest of the people was our job. And I believe wholeheartedly that releasing those parties was not in the best interest of the American people.

—From "The Real S.T."

* * *

Shortly after S.T. was forced to release us, his wife, Rose, asked for a divorce. In a knotted and ironic twist of fate, one of her affairs left her with the sexually transmitted disease herpes, which, it turns out, she passed along to S.T.

S.T.'s STD no doubt played a large role in his stepping down from the government position he held. He did, however, remain in the energy business, and was now working in some position for the CEO of EMCOBP[47]. At this writing, business for S.T.'s company was booming.

Oh, one more thing about S.T.: When Thanloc hacked through his computer to get to Maderwood V's for the launch code to the Plasma Death Ray, he came across a couple of pieces of information about Youvee.

It turns out that S.T. and Peppercorn had a relationship at one time. Or, should I say, S.T. had a relationship with the dominatrix alter-ego Peppercorn used for one of his hustles. Using the screen name "SissyGalinda," S.T. sent to Peppercorn's PayPal account hundreds of dollars, asking the dominatrix to promise to stomp on his testicles and rub his face in doo-doo.

Small world.

Chapter Twenty-Six

Here We Are

As long as I get everything I want, I don't really need much.
—Grey Reflections

As we flew into Lamken, the island looked like a giant world map. The ocean bluer than any blue, an enormous jewel, sparkling. Smaller green and brown land around an oblong-shaped central mass freckled the gem.

We landed without a bump. Thanloc and the others were as silent as I, for all were viewing the island for the first time. I felt an awe from all of them, but wished someone could have pointed things out to me like a tour guide.

Wordlessly, we walked to the door. As soon as I stepped off of the plane, I noticed the air.

It was, perhaps, the most refreshing inhalation I'd ever known, tickled my lungs as if microscopic elves and fairies were playing the harp on my alveoli.

The land was crisp, and looked like it was sprinkled with sugar.

The lushness of the green, the flora, could only have been made with God's own Macbook Pro.

The snow-capped mountains—how could there be snow-capped mountains right in front of me if the temperature was an unbelievably comfortable 78 degrees?—were massive nonpareils.

But the most wonderful sight of all was the people, who had gathered a few hundred yards from the runway. Each was drop-dead, achingly, impossibly gorgeous.

Thanloc said to no-one and everyone, "Here we are."

We were led to a feast. The Elders spoke to us, told much of what I've already said in this book. I heard, in its entirely, Los' vision. They had me believing fairy tales. Because on Lamken, fairy tales come true.

A special seat was reserved for me, next to Wischa. I looked out on a table that seemed not to end, covered with fish, meats, cheeses, vegetables, chocolates, fruit, champagne, wine, caviar, bread—everything that a money-printing machine could buy.

"So, Mr. Grey," Wischa said. "We do not care for details on how you will secure our island. But please keep in mind that anything you need, we will provide. Of course, price is no object. And any laborers you need will also be provided."

"Uh, okay," I said.

"You can relax and enjoy our festival tonight," he said.

"Sounds like a plan."

"Here we are," he said. "Welcome home."

How did I secure Lamken? I built a force-field. I enclosed the entire island in an invisible, protective shell. We were little turtles with no reason to stick out our heads.

"Technology is amazing." That's how I explained the force-field. Few Lamkens have ever asked me, though—they don't care, I guess.

I can't tell you what the force-field is made of. It's a secret, and I don't want the emperor to think he was naked.

* * *

Houses in Lamken aren't gaudy, showy, or massive. Builders are flown in for some of the larger projects. Supplies are imported every day.

I originally requested a rancher, but decided that I wanted a view. So not only did I get a house with a third floor, I had a viewing tower built off of the bedroom. Like a young Pete Townsend, I can see for miles and miles[48].

Everyone who is able helps in the construction of the houses. Nobody has to.

My home is on a bluff. It's not up too high. I've always been a little afraid of heights.

It's not stocked with the latest and greatest technological wonders. I do, though, have a plasma LCD tv. And a nice surround sound system. And comfortable furniture. And a Tempur-pedic bed and pillows. Other than that, I have basic stuff.

Similarly, other Lamkens don't generally want ridiculous amounts of things, perhaps because they can get whatever they want. Power doesn't equal money—the society keeps deferring to the elders[49], because it's their nature. The young respect the old for their wisdom and experience, and the old respect the young for their youth.

I know the Elders would just love Peppercorn. They'd get along like peas in a pod. He would no doubt be made an Elder.

* * *

Welcoming Lamken to the global economy turned out to be an extraordinarily great business Decision for Maderwood V and his colleagues, because a nation with an endless supply of money drove prices of food and energy and wool and fresh water and such even higher.

For a while, many countries around the world didn't accept this nation's money, didn't welcome them to the marketplace. But then they realized how much money they could make on the Lamkens, and gave them the go ahead.

After a few years, nobody had a problem with the Lamkens or their money.

The ironic thing was that if Lamken had any natural resources, or energy to package and sell, the Decision Makers would have shaped their society by helping them sell the goods. They'd have taken an enormous finder's fee, around 99 percent, but would have brought to a select few on the island luxury, technology, and civilization. They'd have introduced poor and rich and inequality, things the Decision Makers believed no civilized society should ever live without.

The Lamkens have not taken—nor ever will take—sides in any global conflict.

By the way, the Lamkens know enough not to think that money could bring people back from the grave, or time travel. They have more sense than that.

The Lamkens learned from the Decision Makers that a lot of things were decided through self interest. The difference is that Lamkens want all selves to have all interests taken care of.

The Decision Makers distance themselves from everyone else. That way, they can't feel anyone's pain. It makes business much easier to conduct.

Lamkens, on the other hand, connect with everyone. People reach out to one another, laugh with each other, cry with each other, love with each other[50]. A group mentality and emotions help shape individuals, and it works well; or at least it has so far. I think that if you have too much one way or another, things collapse. If you have a nice, delicate balance, things work out.

So if people work together for mutual happiness, one can be achieved—as long as the people have all the money they can possibly want.

I've never seen the Lamkens print money. That was probably the only part of the culture that they didn't keep open. Nobody cared about it, though, because everyone got however much everyone wanted. I guess that pretty much debunks the theory that anything that's forbidden will be uncontrollably sexy and cause people to tear down walls to see. As long as people get what they want, why would they care about what's behind that curtain?

* * *

Maybe America's problem is its sex drive. It's so out of control, like a teenager going through a raging puberty, that it needs to fuck everything it sees. And it fucks and fucks so much that it gets too many people pregnant or maybe even contracts a sexually transmitted disease like syphilis and eventually goes crazy.

I still enjoy sex, though I don't crave it nearly as much as I once did. It can't save you. I mean, that's not the answer. I mean, if there is an answer. I'm not even sure of the question.

Epilogue

Here we are.

The Lamkens continued to offer their land to the Decision Makers for their meetings, with only a cost of living increase for the rental rate. The Decision Makers Decided to look for some other real estate.

The Decision Makers, meanwhile, landed on their feet. They always do. They have plenty to cushion their fall.

* * *

I stay current with what's going on in America by reading newspapers, though I do that online now. I can read any newspaper I want—and not just American newspapers, but newspapers all over the world. I read the Philly ones mostly.

I can't get enough local news.

* * *

I still talk to Jeff. When he and Celia divorced, he was devastated. The Elders offered to bring him to Lamken, and he came for a vacation, but didn't stay. He couldn't be apart from his parents.

I know that this story may not paint relationships in the best light, but you may be happy to hear—or, rather, I'm happy to say—that Jeff met someone else and remarried. So it's not true what they say about nice guys not getting the girl.

I do miss him, though. I hoped that he'd move here with his new wife, but I don't anymore. He's happier where he is.

That's all anyone could ask for, isn't it?

I don't miss Vivian anymore, though I do miss things about her. And about us. I miss when she used to say, "Jeez Louise," and when we'd playfully yell at Althea to get off the kitchen table as we ate. She never listened to us.

Gas in the states is at eight bucks a gallon, though that is down from the record high of $9.23 a gallon, which oil companies claimed was a result of the Little League World Series.

In the history of the Lamken society, no one has ever complained about the price of gasoline.

The Lamkens have offered to send me back to America with as much money as I wish, but I haven't yet wanted to leave badly enough.

Tomorrow, though, is always another day.

* * *

I remember the last time Peppercorn appeared to me. It was a couple of years ago, I think. His appearances had become rare. There was less to talk about, I guess, and he always seemed exhausted and in a hurry, like he was coming from a long way.

I don't recall exactly what we talked about. I guess it wasn't that important.

As he was about to ride away, I called out.

"How's heaven?"

He looked over his shoulder, smiled, and said, "What's heaven?"

Then he rode off—into the sunset, of course.

Here we are.

Endnotes

[1] An innovative and immensely successful brewing company whose coffee makers not only ground beans and brewed coffee, but cleaned up after the user was finished.

[2] A reality show where people competed in dance contests. The longer they remained on the show, the more plastic surgery procedures they received.

[3] Fortunately for some and unfortunately for others, physical attributes at this time played a larger role in a person's status than many in the past may have projected.

[4] Not an exact count; my estimation

[5] In the guide, a four-dollar sign ranking was the most expensive

[6] Jeff

[7] The acronym stood for something, but it's not important.

[8] I didn't really know where he could get a deal on livestock. It was a joke that made no sense. At this time in America, people made them all the time.

[9] Remember newspapers? Weren't they great?

[10] Which of course caused the price to rise a bit more

[11] See footnote 8

[12] I have nothing against protein.

[13] A reality show in which 12 contestants are chosen to live in a house for six months. They each are given an allotment of money and are not allowed to bring any other money or work a paying job. They must spend throughout the show, and need to have between one cent and one dollar when the show ends. Viewers vote via text message on which contestant purchased the most wasteful items. Whichever contestant receives the most votes gets to keep not only the items he or she bought, but the items everyone in the house bought.

The ratings for American Idle, incidentally, were astronomical.

[14] A suburb just outside of Philadelphia. The town's slogan is "Everybody's Hometown."

[15] Absolute genius is slightly different than genius

[16] Along with Energy was Land and Home Security, Financial Security, Foreign Affairs Security, and Domestic Security.

[17] A reality show where 20 women vied for Bumper Lovin, a 40-something year old rapper whose song about his 30-inch bumpers, "Me Loves Bumpers," had climbed to number 64 on the charts on the strength of its chorus:

Don't wanna be parking too close to my shit
Cause me bumper loves to bang into shit
Me loves bumpers, bumper bumper hit
And me bumper loves
To bang into shit

The song caused some hard-core fans to put larger and larger bumpers on their cars. There were bumpers so big that some small city streets could only fit a couple of parked cars along each side. A few bumpers even spun, though it was illegal to "bumpflip" while driving.

[18] I hadn't heard a live gunshot since I was 10 or 11, when I went on a hunting trip with my father. We didn't shoot anything but bottles; I don't think he had it in him to kill something, at least not in front of me—and I remember loud, cannon-like blasts coming from the pistol that I was firing.

[19] Even on Lamken, the Decision Makers are male

[20] A trained one

[21] Of course, we had copies at Dubs, and they were available to our customers at $99 each

[22] Again, see Footnote 8

[23] Something that hadn't happened since my trigger-happy teenage years

[24] I, unlike many others at the time, didn't have an IPod or Mp3. I still don't, though price has nothing to do with it. I have a stereo; I sing a lot.

[25] Most likely stupid and certainly forgettable

[26] Aside from the day I was born

[27] Aside from the day I die

[28] D.M.

[29] See Footnote 8

[30] Told you.

[31] The Lamkens have a social networking site as well, called "OurSpace."

[32] With so many more cameras than monitors, some monitors had up to eight channels

[33] I only know the band's name because of her. I never listened to that kind of music before we met, and don't anymore.

[34] Bananas, rice, applesauce and toast

[35] A pressure point hold that brings unconsciousness to the victim within seconds; I do not know how to do it.

[36] In Lamken, hollowed out coconut shells are placed over one's head as a relaxation technique, much like how some breathe into a paper bag.

[37] Fillippo had become a folk hero after his arrest for beating over the head with a chair a man who had siphoned gasoline from his car. Fillippo, who was not a doctor, was found guilty of assault, but before he began serving his sentence choked to death in his holding cell, apparently from a chicken bone.

[38] Fortunately for me, we did not have to travel I-76 on horseback.

[39] A Nintendo Entertainment System game from the 1980s

[40] I said that the Lamken overthrow of the Decision Makers is their only act of treachery. It is. Anyone thinking that what Thanloc did with the poker sites was treacherous is wrong—it simply was poker. Still don't believe me? Ask a real poker player.

[41] I'm aware that it's "shits and giggles"

[42] Much like when I left Julie's, there wasn't much for me to pack, anyway.

[43] Me

[44] "Mushroom Capital of the World," according to Wikipedia and local lore

[45] I never learned how much the reward was; it would have been nice to know what I was worth.

[46] Remember, my mind wasn't exactly clear at this point—I had been seeing my dead friend astride a horse for months

[47] Exxon-Mobil-Conoco-BP

[48] From there; in general, I need my glasses to now see for miles and miles

[49] And the Elders

[50] Not in a free-love, orgy kind of way.